PRAISE FOR

The Taking: Before They Flooded the Quabbin

In the history of Massachusetts, the scale of community displacement for the creation of the Quabbin Reservoir is unparalleled. In *The Taking* the collective, often quiet, suffering brought to bear by government action in the name of "common good" is embodied in the lives of young Josiah, the members of his household, and his community. Helen Haddad has put to words a story that poignantly illustrates the rural New England life of an earlier time. With a keen and personal knowledge of the everyday demands and joys of country living, she has illustrated, through the eyes of a resilient boy, the power of sense of place.

—James French, Department of Conservation and Recreation,
Quabbin, Ware River, and Wachusett Watersheds

"You don't know what you've got 'til it's gone," captures the theme of Helen Haddad's story of loss and renewal. After young Josiah loses his parents to influenza in the 1920s, he is sent to live with his childless aunt and uncle on their farm in the Swift River Valley. But a cloud hovers over the valley—the city he left behind plans to dam the river, flooding all its towns, villages and farms, to supply water to Boston. An unforgettable novel built of evocative detail and depth of human feeling."

—Margo Culley, Professor Emerita of English,
University of Massachusetts, Amherst

History comes alive in Haddad's book, *The Taking: Before They Flooded the Quabbin*. She has seamlessly fitted her historical research into the story of an orphaned boy from Boston in the 1920s. Josiah is uprooted from his home when his parents die and he is sent to live with an aunt and uncle in the Swift River Valley. He has to adjust to living without electricity and running water while he learns about farming. Haddad reminds the reader of the chores young people were required to accomplish every day. Josiah learns to milk cows, feed chickens, make cider and harvest garden produce while going to a one-room school, making friends and warding off the school bully. All during this learning period there are persistent rumors of the ending of the valley to make a reservoir for Boston."

—Dorothy Johnson, author of the *Swift River Anthology*.

"*The Taking* is a finely crafted story revealing the human side of a perplexing episode/event in Massachusetts history. Here historical fiction is served up with a dollop of homesteader "how-to" that will be enjoyed by readers of all ages. This book belongs in every Massachusetts public and school library. It is destined to become a Quabbin area classic."

—Rosemary Heidkamp, Library Director, Wendell Free Library

The Taking:
Before They Flooded the Quabbin

The Taking

Before They Flooded the Quabbin

A Novel

Helen R. Haddad

The Taking: Before they Flooded the Quabbin is a work of fiction set against a historical background. The characters and specific locations are entirely products of the author's imagination. Any resemblance to actual sites or persons, living or dead, is entirely coincidental

Copyright © 2014 Helen R. Haddad

All rights reserved including the right of
reproduction in whole or in part in any form.

Cover art by Helen R. Haddad

Published by *Levellers Press*, Amherst, Massachusetts

Printed in the United States of America

ISBN 978-1-937146-56-6

In memory of J. E. R.

*This book is also for the Swift River Valley that was,
and for all those who were forced to leave it.*

Table of Contents

1	Boston, February 1926	1
2	Leaving	5
3	Starting Over	8
4	Lessons	13
5	Still Learning	19
6	Finding Bessie	24
7	Trip to the Depot	28
8	Wind Storm	32
9	The Icehouse, the Fourth of July, and Ice Cream	37
10	Raspberries, Blueberries, and Fish	42
11	Eggs	47
12	Achilles and Alvin	50
13	Sharpening	53
14	An Arrowhead	57
15	Aunt Ethel's Box	61
16	The Enemy	65
17	Listening on the Stairs	69
18	Back to School	71
19	Apples and Things	78
20	A Whistling Girl	82
21	Fixing Up	85
22	Ready for Winter	89
23	The Letter	93
24	Trees, Turkeys, and Bridges	96
25	Snow, Pigs, and Worry	102
26	A Calf and a Geology Lesson	108

27 The Fight	113
28 Cutting Ice and Another Letter	115
29 Skidding Logs and Josiah Writes	119
30 A Year, Sugaring, and Brave Addy	124
31 Spring and Opportunities	129
32 The Certainty	135
Epilogue	140
Acknowledgments	141

The Swift River... watershed is approximately midway between the seashore at Boston and the western boundary of the State. The preliminary investigation of the State Board of Health in 1895 indicated that a large reservoir could be created in this valley by the construction of a dam...

— Metropolitan Water Supply Report of 1922

1
Boston, February 1926

EACH CLACK OF THE WHEELS ON THE TRAIN TRACK was like a fresh slap of reality for Josiah. He still couldn't believe what had happened, and now he was going to a place he knew nothing about, a place where he didn't belong.

He thought back to that terrible afternoon—how could it be only six days ago?—when everything started to change. He came home from school and found his mother trembling from a chill—his mother who was almost never sick. "I'm glad you're home," she said weakly, but usually she asked him all about his day.

"I'll make tea to chase away this chill," she said, getting up from her chair. After she fixed the tea, the sound of the teacup rattling against the saucer filled Josiah's head. He watched as she started back to her rocking chair, and saw the cup slip off its saucer, plunge to the floor, and break into pieces. Little rivers of tea ran across the floor.

"Oh!" she exclaimed, her shaking hand still holding the empty saucer.

Josiah hurried over to help clean up the mess. "I'll save the pieces," he said. "Maybe we can glue them back together."

She shook her head. He set them aside anyway. It was the blue-and-white cup that had belonged to her mother, and he knew it meant something to her. I'll match up the pieces later, he thought.

She turned toward her bedroom. "I just need to lie down for a bit," she said. "I'll be fine."

But she wasn't fine. As her fever climbed, she threw off the warm blanket that Josiah had gotten for her earlier, the gray one with the fringe. She didn't get up to start fixing supper. Josiah watched the minute hand on the mantle clock jerk forward as he waited for his pa to come home from work. Later Pa dipped cloths into cold water and put them on Ma's forehead. She started to cough, and during the night her cough, rasping in her chest like a saw, woke Josiah. He wanted to stop it, but he couldn't help her; all he could do was put his hands over his ears.

In the morning she was worse, and Pa was sick, too. Pa sent for the doctor and let Josiah stay home from school. When the doctor came with his black bag and stethoscope, he examined them and announced that it was influenza. "You must both stay quietly in bed and drink plenty of fluids," he directed.

Josiah brought them water and mopped their fevered brows. He felt odd touching his father this way, caring for his parents. And nothing that he did lessened their violent coughing spasms. *They're not getting better*, he realized, *they're even sicker. It can't go on like this. It can't.*

At last the doctor came again, and he insisted that Ma and Pa should be in the hospital. "I can take you there in my auto," he added.

Between fits of coughing, Pa agreed to go. "Mrs. Potts, who lives downstairs, can come to stay the night with Josiah," he told the doctor.

Josiah made a face at the mention of Mrs. Potts, but at least he wouldn't have to listen to the terrible coughing. He felt relieved and guilty all at once as he watched them being taken away.

That night Josiah lay awake in the quiet dark, thinking of nurses taking care of his parents and that soon they would be well enough to come home.

In the morning the apartment felt strange. Mrs. Potts made lumpy oatmeal for breakfast, bustling about in his mother's kitchen as if she belonged there. "I'm not hungry," he told her. His ma's oatmeal never had lumps. Mrs. Potts was washing the stuck oatmeal out of the pot when there was a loud knocking at the door. Josiah went and opened it, finding the doctor standing on the landing with his hat in his hand.

"My poor boy," the doctor said, reaching his other hand out toward Josiah. "They are both gone."

"Gone?" Josiah asked. "Gone where?"

"Gone to Heaven," the doctor answered.

"No!" Josiah exclaimed. "No. That can't be true."

The doctor put his hand on Josiah's shoulder. "I'm sorry, very sorry, but your parents both died."

A coldness seemed to start in Josiah's feet, creeping upward until he felt entirely numb, almost frozen, unable to say anything. He heard Mrs. Potts screaming right behind him, and yet it seemed she was miles away.

BY AFTERNOON, NEIGHBORS FILLED THE APARTMENT, talking about the great Spanish flu epidemic of 1918, only eight years before. Someone had brought little, plain cakes, and Mrs. Potts brewed bitter coffee. They said things like "such a pity" and "at least they're together." After that they talked about him. Couldn't they see that he had ears on the sides of his head?

"What a miracle that the boy didn't take sick. But what will become of him?" they wondered.

"Kind of a quiet, skinny boy," a man said. "Who'd want him?"

Suddenly, this new problem came crashing over Josiah like a wave. Where would he go? He tried not to listen, but he couldn't shut out the voices around him.

"How old is he, anyway?" inquired a neighbor.

"Twelve or so, I think. We can't take him in, with seven to feed already," a woman from the next building answered. "Doesn't he have any close kin?"

"I'm sure the minister will know," someone said. "Or the doctor or the hospital—they'll know who to notify."

"I have an aunt. My mother's older sister," Josiah announced, and everyone stopped talking. Immediately he wished he'd kept his mouth shut. He'd never met his aunt, who lived with her husband to the west somewhere, on a farm. Probably she wouldn't want him, and he didn't want to leave Boston. He just wanted to run out of the dark apartment with its shades all drawn, down the stairs, and out into the street. He would run and run, away from everything, run until he woke up from this nightmare. How could he believe, really believe, that he would never, ever see his parents again?

That night Mrs. Potts said that she would stay, but he didn't want her there, putting her arm around him as if he were five, with the smell of her, like old, overcooked cabbage, too close. "I'll be all right alone," he told her. "There's nothing you can do for me."

She fussed over him, trying to get him to eat some of the soup she had brought upstairs. Josiah picked up the spoon and put it down again, sure he would vomit if he tried even one spoonful of the greasy broth. She clucked her tongue. "Well, I'm only one floor down if you need me."

Josiah was glad to hear the door click closed, glad to hear the heaviness of her feet on the steps. But then he was left alone with the silence.

He went into the bathroom, used the toilet, and pulled the chain to flush. Water gurgled down the pipe from the overhead tank and swirled in the bowl. He found himself staring at the bathtub, at its claw feet, as if they were gripping him. He shook his head and went over to the sink, washed his hands, and splashed hot water up at his face.

Wandering about the apartment, he wondered what would happen to him. They had moved before, three times that he remembered, but always together, always in Boston. He had never been anywhere but Boston, unless you counted day trips to Nantasket Beach, or one to Salem. He didn't have any relatives here, he knew that. So unless his aunt took him, where would he go? He felt as if he were standing unbalanced on the edge of a cliff above a giant, black whirlpool. He shook himself—too much imagination, that's what Ma would say.

After pacing back and forth and listening to the nearby church bell strike the hours, he decided to go to bed. He switched off the electric lamp and lay still in the darkness. The bell sounded again, just one strike this time, and Josiah found sobs coming so fast he could hardly breathe between them.

2
Leaving

BEFORE THE FUNERAL STARTED, WHILE A FEW FRIENDS and acquaintances were gathering at the church, the minister told Josiah not to worry. "Your parents were taken from you, but they are safe in Heaven, and surely there will be a place for you to go here on this earth."

Clenching his teeth, Josiah didn't answer. Did the minister mean in an orphanage, or placed, like one boy in his class at school, as an unwanted foster child? Josiah imagined a crowded dormitory full of underfed boys, or— He stopped himself; better not to imagine. Had anyone gotten word to his aunt, telling her that his parents were dead? When he asked, no one knew. Well, he thought, I'm not dead, so I'll have to go somewhere.

Josiah sat alone in the front pew of the church, trying not to fidget. Just as the service began, a man and a woman he had never seen before hurried into the other end of the pew. Josiah looked more closely and realized that the woman must be his aunt. She had graying hair and was tall and spare where his mother had been short and rounded. Still, she looked like his mother, and seeing her made the empty place inside him hurt.

The woman looked over at him and gave a little gasp, but by then Josiah was busy trying to wall everything out, determined to keep himself from crying in public. He could still hear his father's voice—it had been when he was only five or six—saying, "You're old enough now not to cry, so keep a stiff upper lip." He swallowed hard and kept the tears from coming.

At the cemetery, after the minister said his final words, earth thudded down on the coffins. Josiah stood unmoving, looking at the mound of earth, until, for the second time, the minister said, "We must go now." As they walked away, toward the gate, he heard his aunt— he remembered now that her name was Ethel—say to the minister, "My only sister's only child, of course we'll take him."

"The boy will be a help to you on the farm, another pair of hands, since you don't have any children," the minister responded.

So they will take me, Josiah thought. I will go to live with my aunt and uncle on a farm. It was settled, and for a moment his spirits rose. But how could this all be decided without even asking him? I don't want to go, he thought. I don't want to live in the country. He looked down at his hands, thinking that they wouldn't be much help.

Wishing that he knew more about this farm, since he was going there, he wondered why his ma hardly ever talked about it. Was it because his father was from the city, from Boston? He remembered once hearing his pa say to his ma, "You're lucky I rescued you from spending your life on that farm." And now that's where he was going. Backwards.

VERY EARLY THE NEXT DAY, they finished packing up his few belongings. Josiah slid in the picture of his mother and father, smiling so happily at each other on their wedding day. He also took his three favorite books and a few school notebooks—one half-filled with drawings he had made of buildings, autos, and faces.

Aunt Ethel put linens, blankets, and some china that had once belonged to her mother into a trunk. She wrapped the pieces of the broken teacup in some paper, stuffed them into a corner of the trunk, and closed the lid. "Aren't we going to take anything else, at least my mother's rocking chair?" Josiah asked.

"No," Aunt Ethel answered. "It's been decided. I'm afraid everything will have to be sold to pay for the funeral and the hospital."

"Then I'm not going," Josiah exploded angrily. "That was Ma's favorite chair, and I'm not going to leave it for strangers to sit in." For a moment he glared at his aunt as if everything were her fault, even though he knew it wasn't.

"I see," Aunt Ethel said, but there was a surprised look on her face, as if she had hoped to eat something sweet and instead it was sour. "I'll speak to Uncle Perry about the chair."

He heard them talking in the kitchen. "You know how I've missed my sister ever since she left the farm—and now she's gone forever. And the boy, he . . ." She stopped, leaving her words hanging in the air.

Soon everything was ready and the door was locked behind them. They walked down the stairs, three flights. Josiah held his bag, remembering how, when he was little, his ma always made him hold her hand, and how sometimes they had laughed and counted the steps together.

A neighbor drove them to the train station in his new motorcar. The trunk was strapped on behind and the rocking chair was tied to the roof. Josiah squeezed himself against the car door so as not to bump Uncle Perry. They passed his school. Some boys were already playing in the schoolyard, and for a moment he wanted to wave good-bye, even though he didn't know them. His eyes fixed on the crowded bustle of the Boston streets, lined with dirty snow, and on the people hurrying along the sidewalks. I am going to the middle of nowhere, he thought. I won't know anybody, and I won't know what to do there.

The automobile pulled up at the station, and they all got out. "I wish we could stay longer to finish settling everything," Uncle Perry told the man as he thanked him for the ride. "But there are the cows to milk, I've got to tap the maples, and I gave my word that we'd be back today."

Cows, thought Josiah. I hope they won't expect me to milk a cow.

Then the three of them were on the train—a real train, not a street railway car or a trolley. Josiah thought of how he used to beg his parents to take him on a real train trip. If only they were here, this would feel like an adventure, like his lucky day.

He looked at Aunt Ethel and Uncle Perry sitting stiff in their seats, their mouths straight lines. Did they think they had made a mistake, agreeing to take him? Was that why they weren't saying anything? He knew he should thank them—for taking the rocking chair, for taking him in—but he couldn't seem to begin. The whistle blew, the train lurched forward, and the wheels began clacking on the rails. They left Boston behind, heading west, west to the Swift River Valley.

3

Starting Over

"How far is it from Boston?" Josiah asked as the train left the city and began to move through farmland. It might as well be to the ends of the earth, he thought.

"About sixty miles as the crow flies, but longer by train," his aunt answered. Josiah stared out the window for a while, watching houses, fields, and trees all blur together. The journey stretched on and on, the train whistle blowing as they came to crossings or stopped at towns, each one farther from Boston. And when they arrived, when they reached this farm, what would his aunt and uncle expect from him?

"Ours is the next stop," Aunt Ethel said, and then the conductor called out, "Enfield! Enfield. All out for Enfield." Josiah felt the train jolt and heard the hissing of its brakes. He wondered where they went from here, how close the farm was.

"Hurry up now." Uncle Perry's words cut into his thoughts. "We don't want to keep Mr. Damon waiting."

Josiah grabbed his bag and stepped off the train behind his aunt and uncle. He saw Uncle Perry go over to a man standing with a horse and sled, and he guessed that the man must be Mr. Damon. They had to wait while boxes, the trunk, and the rocker came off the train. Josiah watched steam rise from a pile of manure that the big horse dropped into the snow.

A man came up, stopping next to his aunt. "Sorry to hear about your sister," he said.

"Thank you, Chub," Aunt Ethel replied, giving a quick nod.

"Heard you had to go all the way to Boston. I get mad every time I think of Boston, of what they might do to us. Mind my words, they'll go ahead and decide to build the dam, no matter what we say."

"I don't want to speak about that now," she said firmly, leaving Josiah to wonder why it should matter if Boston built a dam. Boston was so far away. Maybe something about taxes—people always complained about taxes, his pa used to say.

The man moved away as the sled was loaded. They set off and soon left the town behind. At first the road was fairly level and the horse trotted along briskly. "This is the bottom of the river valley. It's flatter here, and the soil is better—and not so full of rocks," Aunt Ethel told him, as if the information should mean something to him.

Later they turned uphill. "Our farm is up in the hills, not in Enfield," Aunt Ethel explained. "How much farther?" Josiah asked. "A fair bit more," she answered.

Soon the road followed beside a fast-moving stream. A layer of snow spread over fields, woods, and scattered farms. At last the horse turned off the road, and Josiah saw a house tucked against the side of a hill, with a great barn rising beside it.

As soon as their things were unloaded, with the trunk brought in and the rocking chair set in the parlor, Uncle Perry went straight to the barn, saying something about cows and work to be done. Josiah and Aunt Ethel were left standing together in the kitchen. "Colder here than in the barn," she said, lifting a lid on the wood-burning kitchen range. "Fire's out, but I'll get us warmed up soon," she added, looking at her nephew. Josiah shivered, and she put her arms out to hug him, but he took a step away. "I guess you want to be left alone for a bit," she said.

"I don't want anything," Josiah mumbled, realizing that he did want something; he wanted to be back home in Boston with his parents alive, something he couldn't say. He watched silently as his aunt shook down the stove grates and took some small sticks of wood from the box of kindling by the stove.

Once the fire was going, Aunt Ethel told Josiah to bring his bag and she would show him his room. He followed her up the narrow stairs and into a small room with part of the ceiling following the slant of the roof. "This used to be your Uncle Albert's room," she said.

"Who was Uncle Albert?" he asked.

She looked at him dumbfounded, her jaw dropping. "Why, my brother, of course. Your ma's brother, your uncle!"

"My uncle? You mean I've had an uncle for my whole life, and I didn't even know it? I never heard of him, never," Josiah insisted. Why hadn't his ma ever even told him that she had a brother? What else didn't he know? "Where is Uncle Albert now? Can I meet him?"

"No, you can't," Aunt Ethel replied, answering his second question. She had a shocked look, as if his words had hit her like fists. She shook her head, turned away, and moved out of the room. Turning back at the top of the stairs, she said, "I'll let you get settled while I set to fixing supper."

Alone, Josiah looked around the room quickly—a narrow bed, a small chest of drawers, a washstand with a bowl and pitcher, a straight chair, and two small-paned windows. Uncle Albert's room. But what had happened to his Uncle Albert? Was he dead, too? Clearly, Aunt Ethel didn't want to tell him anything, and right now he had a different problem.

Where was the bathroom? He looked into the room across the hall, maybe his mother's old room, and into a closet. Nothing. As he started down the stairs, he remembered his ma saying something about an old privy, and how glad she was to leave that behind. Wasn't there any bathroom? No flush toilet, no indoor plumbing in the whole house?

Aunt Ethel looked up as he hurried into the kitchen. "The privy?" she questioned.

Josiah nodded. "Out beyond the barn," she said, pointing to the door. He unlatched it quickly and, pulling his coat together to shut out the wind, made for the first small building he saw. After fumbling with the hook, he found himself confronted by a flock of clucking chickens. He slammed the door and struggled to rehook it. Looking up, he saw a dog bounding toward him, barking. Josiah raced to a smaller building; its door creaked open on rusting hinges, just in time. An old wooden toilet seat was before him, set into a sort of bench, and a little box filled with sheets of rough paper hung on the wall. He was safe from the dog, but a definite stench assaulted his nostrils as the cold air gusted up out of the seat.

When he came out, the dog was waiting. It reared up in front of him, barking fiercely, teeth bared. His back to the privy door, Josiah stood transfixed. Would the dog chase him and bite him if he made a run for the house? The shaggy, black-and-tan dog stood on its hind legs, holding him at bay. He'd never had to deal with animals in Boston, had never had a pet. The dog's teeth looked sharper with each bark.

Suddenly, Uncle Perry came out of the barn. "Quiet, Shep. Quiet! Come!" he called. Obediently, the dog turned and went to sit by Uncle Perry. "Now you come here, Josiah."

He came, but more slowly than the dog, and stood on the other side of Uncle Perry.

"This is Shep. He's a fool dog, but he won't hurt you. Now hold out your hand and let him smell you," Uncle Perry ordered.

Josiah extended his hand hesitantly and was surprised by the cold wet of the dog's black nose. He drew his hand back quickly.

"See, his tail's wagging now," Uncle Perry said. "Guess he likes you. Go tell your aunt I'll be along soon." With a backward glance at Shep, Josiah went into the house.

THEY ATE A SIMPLE SUPPER AT THE KITCHEN TABLE, near the warmth of the wood-burning stove. Josiah said he didn't want anything, but Aunt Ethel made him drink a glass of fresh milk and eat a hot biscuit. Nobody said much. He remembered his ma telling him that people didn't talk much where she grew up, that they didn't like to "waste words on idle conversation." But, Josiah told himself, they must be thinking even if they're not talking. I'm always thinking about something. I can't just turn my mind off, even if I'm quiet.

Before bed, Josiah realized that he needed to make another trip to the privy. Aunt Ethel saw him open the door and look out into the dark. "Here," she said, "as the moon's not up, take a kerosene lantern to light your way."

The circle of lantern light helped, and Shep, wherever he was, did not come and bark. Josiah thought back to Boston, thought about the electric lights he had switched on and off so easily, the central heating warming each room, and the simple flush of the toilet—all gone.

I'll never get used to this, he thought, to being on this farm, to them. And his aunt, not to mention Uncle Perry, who wasn't even really related to him—would they get used to him, even get to like him? Would he measure up?

When he came in with the lantern, Josiah saw Shep lying on the floor, his tail thumping. Aunt Ethel was by the stove, and in the soft lantern light she reminded him once more of his mother. He felt a tightness in his throat and looked around the room to avoid looking at his aunt. His eyes caught the back of Ma's rocker. Was nothing safe?

Something brushed against his leg. He jumped aside, setting the lantern swinging, as a striped cat bounded across the room.

"That's only Tiger, my house cat," she explained. "He's a good mouser."

Feeling sheepish, Josiah dropped his gaze to the still-swaying lantern in his hand.

"The chimney needs cleaning," his aunt remarked. Josiah glanced at the stovepipe rising through the kitchen ceiling, and then toward the old fireplace in the parlor and the mantelpiece above it. Finally he said, "The chimney in the parlor? How can you tell it needs cleaning?"

Aunt Ethel gave him a quick smile. "I mean the glass chimney on the lantern. I need to clean the soot off it and trim the wick. Here," she said, handing him a candle in a holder in exchange for the lantern. "Take this for light going up the stairs." She took a match and lit the candle for him.

Josiah felt so tired he wondered how he managed to climb the steps. The candle threw strange, flickering shadows about the room, looming up the walls. He tried to imagine a boy named Albert in this room. What was he like, and what had happened to him? Josiah blew out the flame and tugged the worn blanket and warm patchwork quilt tight around himself. Soon he was asleep in Uncle Albert's old bed.

4
Lessons

When he woke up the next morning in the small, chill room, it took Josiah a moment to figure out where he was, even to remember that his parents were dead.

He dressed quickly, nearly tripped over his feet coming down the steep steps, and nodded to Aunt Ethel in the warm kitchen before rushing out into the cold to the privy. On his way back he saw Uncle Perry, with Shep by his side, filling buckets with water from an old hand pump. "Morning," his uncle called out, and Shep didn't bark.

"Morning," Josiah replied, wondering how much water had to be pumped each day. Back in the kitchen, Aunt Ethel told him that he could have a day or two to get used to the farm and learn about chores before going back to school. Josiah swallowed and said, "Yes, ma'am." The only chores he'd ever done in Boston were carrying packages for his mother and shining his father's shoes. He'd quite forgotten about going to a new school. One more hoop to jump through, he thought.

"After breakfast I'll show you the henhouse and then the dairy. We'll make butter today, so you can help with the churning, and then there's kindling to be split for the stove. Uncle Perry is busy tapping the maple trees. He'll show you about that and the cows, pigs, horses, and what's where in the barn later."

Josiah felt dizzy. They couldn't expect him to do chores for all those things, could they? Maybe Uncle Albert had hated doing chores and had run away from home. But at least Uncle Albert grew up on a farm, this very farm, and so he knew how to do things like split kindling. I don't know how to do any of it, he thought. I'll have to learn everything from scratch.

Before the end of the day, he had made an exhausting list in his head of dos and don'ts, everything from how to get eggs out from under a hen without being pecked to how to prime the pump after he had dumped it by mistake. He hadn't even known what it meant to dump a pump. He guessed he wouldn't do that again, leaving the long pump handle up instead of down, allowing the water to "dump" inside the pump so that no matter how hard he pumped, no water came out of the spout. His arm was still sore from trying.

Aunt Ethel was patient about the pump, didn't scold, and showed him how to prime it—how to get it going again—by pouring water into the top of it. Nevertheless, she sometimes seemed as perplexed as he was about how to proceed, about where to begin—there was so much she had to explain. He wondered if his aunt and uncle would soon wish, if they didn't already, that he were in some orphanage in Boston.

By the time Uncle Perry finished showing him about the barn, sheds, and sugarhouse the next day, he was beginning to lose track of everything. When Uncle Perry said, "It's a busy time because of the sugaring, and we'll be boiling soon," what did that mean? At least some of the things Uncle Perry told him were only warnings—he hadn't set the barn on fire or let the pigs loose, at least not yet. Twice Uncle Perry said, "You don't know anything about anything, do you"—but he said it with a kind, puzzled expression.

How could I have thought there would be nothing to do here? he asked himself. And tomorrow he would go to a new school. Maybe that would be better than being on the farm, or maybe, as his ma used to say, he'd be jumping out of the frying pan and into the fire. Anyway, he suddenly realized, he would be expected to do chores and go to school.

He tried to put all of the pieces together. The picture they made still had so many parts missing. Where did he, Josiah, fit in, if he ever could fit in here?

HIS REGULAR SCHOOL CLOTHES SEEMED OUT OF PLACE as he put them on, reminding him of home, of Boston, and of his parents—of how Ma said good-bye to him each morning as he left for school, and of how his father quizzed him about his lessons in the evening.

After breakfast Aunt Ethel packed him a lunch pail, laced up her boots, and walked with him down the rutted but still frozen road all the way to the schoolhouse. Half of him wished she'd stayed home, and the other half didn't.

"I went to this school," she said, "and so did your ma and, of course, your Uncle Albert, though Albert didn't do much studying. It's only got one room and one teacher, but it was a good school then."

Unable to contain his curiosity, Josiah asked, "What happened to Uncle Albert?"

"Well, he left."

"Left?"

"Yes, he did" was all the response Aunt Ethel gave. At least he was alive when he left, Josiah thought, that's something.

"I expect you to do your lessons and do what the teacher says," she added, as if she expected that he might not. Josiah guessed that Uncle Albert hadn't.

They turned in at the gate and plowed through a group of pupils as Aunt Ethel headed straight for the teacher. Josiah hung back, glancing around at the other boys and girls. He missed the clamor of the Irish and Italian boys in the Boston schoolyard, thinking of the classmates he hadn't said good-bye to at his old school.

Later the teacher, Miss Cooper, introduced him: "We have a new pupil today. Josiah has come all the way from Boston to live here in the Swift River Valley. I'm sure that you will make him welcome." But when Miss Cooper turned toward the blackboard, chalk in hand, he felt something hit his neck. It fell forward into his lap—an enormous spitball. Some welcome, Josiah thought.

Miss Cooper found a few books for him and told him to start at the beginning of each. Someone had written answers in the arithmetic book, and he saw right away that half of them were wrong. Then he looked at the reader: it was an old copy of the one he had read the year before last. He raised his hand, but the teacher didn't seem to see it. His arm started to sag. "Excuse me," he said. "Could I have some different books?"

"When you have completed all the exercises in those books, then you may ask that question," she replied. A ripple of giggles ran through the room; even the younger pupils were laughing at the "new boy." Josiah turned red in the face and tried to look as if he didn't care. At recess one of the bigger boys called him "Boston" and "Water Boy." Later a volley of spitballs hit him. The day dragged. How could he concentrate in a school like this?

At last Miss Cooper rang the bell for dismissal and it was time for him to walk back to the farm. At first there were several others walking his way, and then there was only one, a girl. After a few minutes she told him that she would be walking almost the whole way to and from school with him each day because her farm was right next to his aunt and uncle's. She wasn't like the girls in Boston, who didn't talk to boys. "What's your whole name?" she asked. "Mine's Adelaide Hortense Isabel Damon." He didn't answer, not expecting to have a conversation with a scraggly girl. "Well, what is it?" she insisted.

He told her, just so she would leave him alone. "Josiah Johnson Wallace."

But she didn't leave him alone. "Do they call you Joe?" she asked.

"No, they don't," he replied. He wasn't sure that he really liked his name, but it wasn't a common name, and he liked that, and he liked knowing that it had once belonged to his grandfather Josiah Johnson.

"Everybody calls me Addy," she announced. "You know that big boy who turned off first? The one who was sitting behind you? He puts stones in his spitballs, and his name is Alvin Slade. The Slades have a really big farm and the most cows. And the Pratt boys, the ones who turned off next, they're named Tom and Nat, and they stick together close as bread and butter. But they never yank my braids or bother people, not like Alvin."

Josiah didn't say anything, and they kept on walking. Suddenly, Addy stopped right in front of him. Softly, she said, "I'm sorry about your parents. My ma and pa, they knew your mother when they were all young, before she went to Boston, and they told me. So I'm sorry." She stood there, looking at him with her green-blue eyes.

"Thank you," he said, rather stiffly. "I don't want to talk about it."

"Oh, I'm sorry," Addy repeated, and they walked a bit in silence. "Are you a loner? My pa says that your uncle, Albert, was a loner."

"What do you mean, a loner?"

"You know, it's someone who doesn't do what everybody else does," Addy replied, looking him right in the eyes. "Someone independent. Maybe I'm a bit of a loner, but Ma says that I'm just a tomboy and she hopes I'll grow past it soon. I'll never be like my older sister, Betty, though—she would never do anything that all the other girls don't do."

Josiah hesitated, thinking. Independent? Yes, that fit. And he didn't always want to go along with what all the other boys wanted to do at his last school. Maybe he was a loner, like Uncle Albert. "I really don't know anything about my uncle; in fact, I never knew about him at all until I came here," Josiah said, wondering why he was telling Addy this, when he usually kept his thoughts to himself.

"Everybody knows that he went out west, but I don't know exactly when or where or why. You should ask your aunt."

"I did, but she doesn't want to talk about it."

At school everyone pretty much ignored him after the first few days, even Miss Cooper—everyone except for Addy, and Alvin. Once Alvin and the Pratt boys turned off the road, Addy would start asking questions. "Why do you think Miss Cooper doesn't like questions?" she wanted to know.

A few days later, he asked Addy why Alvin and some of the other boys kept calling him "Boston" and "Water Boy."

"Because you're from Boston, and Boston's running out of water," Addy answered.

"What do you mean? There was always plenty of water in Boston."

She was quiet for a minute before she asked, "Do you think they'll really dam up the Swift River and flood the whole valley, all our farms and the towns, too?"

"I don't know how or why anybody would," he replied, wondering what she would imagine next. Until he'd met Addy, he'd thought he had a lot of imagination, but this took the cake.

"Well, I guess you don't want to talk about the dam, either. Lots of people don't. I suppose you know about the plans, though, being from Boston, so you know it's all because of enemy domain."

"Enemy? What enemy? Sounds like a crazy idea to me," Josiah replied.

"It is a crazy idea, but my pa says that the people in Boston are going to take our land and build the dam anyhow. I can't help thinking about it, thinking it might happen, with the water rising, and we'll all have to move."

Without thinking, Josiah answered, "Maybe your pa is crazy."

Addy stamped her foot and walked faster, not saying another word. Then Josiah remembered the man at the train depot in Enfield. What had he said about Boston and a dam? Maybe Addy wasn't making things up. He'd ask his aunt and uncle about all of it tonight.

They were at the table in the kitchen, finishing supper, with nobody talking. "I heard that there is a plan to build a dam on the river. Is that true?" Josiah asked.

Uncle Perry looked at Aunt Ethel and said nothing. Aunt Ethel said, "We don't speak of damming the river in this house." And that was the end of it.

Why not speak of it? What was it that she wouldn't talk about? At least now he knew that Addy hadn't made it all up. But the next day when he asked Addy about the dam, he got nowhere. "You said my pa was crazy, and you didn't want to talk about it, so I won't," she retorted.

"But I didn't understand. I didn't know it might matter."

"Well, now you do know. It matters. But right now I don't want to talk about it," Addy replied, still in a huff. She tossed her head back, flinging her braids so that he could hear them slap against her back.

So nobody would tell him anything. Unanswered questions spun in his head—Uncle Albert and the flooding of the valley blurring together like the colors on a spinning top.

5
Still Learning

He knew that Aunt Ethel and Uncle Perry tried to "make allowances," but he also knew he wasn't much help. He certainly wasn't any help with the sugaring—not strong enough to carry the big buckets full of maple sap. There was so much to remember. He'd never worked so hard or been so tired in his life. The days all banged together like cars being added to a freight train. Once he overheard Uncle Perry say to Aunt Ethel, "I tell him how to do things, but it must go in one ear and right out the other. Sometimes I wonder if we made a mistake, taking him."

"We've got to give the boy more time," she answered. "It's a change for all of us. He'll do better."

There were other things Josiah tried hard not to remember. He still avoided even looking at his ma's rocker, because it reminded him of her too much. And he kept his parents' wedding picture facedown in a drawer.

One morning before breakfast, Uncle Perry said, "It's time you learned to milk a cow."

Do I have to? Josiah wanted to answer. He'd known this was coming, and he'd already put it off as long as possible. While he'd gotten used to Shep and the cats, the hens, and even the pigs, and maybe the horses, he was never sure what the cows, with their tossing horns and shifting hooves, might do next. I can't say no, he thought, so he nodded a silent "yes." They went out to the barn, and soon Josiah was facing the back end of a cow. He watched while Uncle Perry milked. Then it was his turn.

"First, wash off Spangle's milk bag good, the way I just showed you with Rosie," Uncle Perry instructed. "Then try milking her."

Spangle turned her head around and looked at Josiah as he scrubbed her udder, very gingerly at first, wondering how he could really be doing this. The cow kept swiping her rough tongue in and out of her mouth. Then she let go with a big, semi-liquid splop of manure. Most of it landed in the gutter behind her, ready to be shoveled down one of the small trapdoors in the gutter's floor, but some dribbled down her hind legs. If Uncle Perry hadn't been standing there watching him, he would have bolted out of the barn right then. Instead, he washed the cow off all over again.

As soon as he got down beside her and settled on the three-legged milking stool, Spangle whipped her tail across his face. She doesn't like me, he thought.

"Time to start milking, slow and steady," Uncle Perry directed.

So he made himself reach out and grasp her teats the way Uncle Perry had showed him. He squeezed, and a bit of milk dribbled into the pail. He gripped the rubbery teats harder and harder, but less and less milk came out. The cow gazed at him with her soft, brown eyes. Then, before Josiah realized what she was up to, Spangle kicked over the pail. The stool went out from under him, and he landed in the manure-filled gutter.

Josiah wished he had never, ever come to live on a farm—even an orphanage would have been better!

IT WAS APRIL NOW, WITH THE GROUND THAWING, buds swelling, and mud deepening in the barnyard and on the road—"mud season," Aunt Ethel called it. Josiah was doing better with his chores. Milking cows still could be a challenge, but he'd gotten the knack of it, although he avoided milking Spangle if possible. When he split a whole armload of kindling and filled the box by the stove, there was something satisfying about having done the job, and Aunt Ethel gave him a smile. He thought she smiled more than she had when he'd first come. Or was he just getting used to the way she was?

Life was so different here, bigger and smaller all at once—it stretched across fields, up hills and down rutted roads, full of chores and new ways to do things, and yet it was also stuck in a simple sameness, all hemmed in. Sometimes he thought about the business and bustle of Boston, of people rushing past, and wished that at least he was back in his old school.

While he'd learned a lot of lessons on the farm, school was worse than boring. It was as if he had been dropped back a grade or two for no reason. Even reading, always his favorite subject, had lost its flavor. Beyond that, he didn't have any friends. He liked Addy, even though she was sometimes prickly, but could a girl really be a friend?

The Pratt boys seemed a self-sufficient unit, and the other boys, well, they took their cues from Alvin. As for Alvin, Josiah minded Alvin more and more. The stones in the spitballs were sharp, and Alvin was good at tripping him, jabbing him with an elbow, and making Josiah spill his ink or drop his schoolbooks. He sneered and called Josiah "Boston" or "Boston Boy" as if that were his name. While Alvin called Addy "Carrot Head" and Dick Hutchins was always "Slowpoke," he concentrated on Josiah for more than name-calling.

One morning Josiah was so absorbed in a drawing he was making of Miss Cooper that he didn't notice Alvin looking over his shoulder. Suddenly a hand reached out and snatched the drawing. Alvin sniggered, waving his prize in the air.

"Alvin Slade, what's so funny? Give me that paper," the teacher demanded.

"But it's not my paper. The Boston boy drew it," Alvin answered, handing it over. Miss Cooper stared at his drawing. Josiah watched as her eyebrows clamped together. He'd exaggerated everything—her goggle glasses, the stray hairs jutting from her chin, her wrinkles and pinched mouth. She crumpled the paper.

"Josiah, you will get an F for this week," she snapped. "And you will write 'I will not draw in school' one hundred times." She walked over to the potbellied stove, opened the loading door, and tossed in his drawing.

Pretend you don't care, Josiah told himself for the hundredth time—that worked at the last school. Pretend that you don't want to punch Alvin and that you don't hate this school. He stared down at his desk.

After school Addy was waiting for him by the gate. "Your drawing must have been pretty good for Miss Cooper to get that upset about it," she remarked. "I wish I could have seen it. Would you let me see one sometime?"

"Sometime," Josiah answered, feeling pleased with himself for a moment. Drawing was a thing he could do, even if today it had gotten him into trouble—something he wouldn't tell Aunt Ethel about.

SUDDENLY MUD SEASON WAS OVER AND SPRING ARRIVED. Rushing and bubbling, the water in the brook overflowed its banks, then receded. As the fields turned green, Addy bubbled with questions. "Why can't people eat grass the way cows can?" she wanted to know.

"Because a cow has four stomachs and can bring the food back up from its rumen, that's its first stomach, and chew its cud. Then the cow swallows the cud down again and it goes to the next stomach, and so on until the grass is digested," he answered—glad that he had looked at Uncle Perry's tattered copy of *The Dairy Farmer's Guide*, glad to be able to tell Addy what he'd learned.

"Well, I only have one stomach," Addy said. "Now I know what cows are doing when they chew, but why does a robin build its nest with mud and a phoebe bird with moss?"

A few days later, while Uncle Perry turned the dirt in the kitchen garden with a digging fork, Josiah watched hungry, red-breasted robins hop about in the newly dug earth, seizing exposed worms and tugging them out of the rich, dark soil. The sight of a bird nearly falling over backwards, yanking at a big, stretching worm, made Josiah laugh out loud, something he realized he hadn't done for a long while. Then he heard himself asking one of Addy's questions: "Where do robins go, exactly, during the winter?"

"South," Uncle Perry answered.

"But where in the South?" Josiah persisted, sounding like Addy.

"Don't rightly know. I've got other things to worry about."

Josiah found that it was harder to worry about things in spring. Walking to school one morning when everything was wet with raindrops, he saw the sun burst out from between clouds and change the raindrops into tiny, sparkling rainbows. Josiah, Addy, and the Pratt boys all stopped, their lunch pails banging against their legs, just to look at the magic of it. Addy broke the spell. "How does the sun change the water into colors?" she asked. Nobody answered.

When the last day of spring term came at the end of May, just before Memorial Day, Josiah was more than glad that school was over. There was a little ceremony with everyone standing outside the schoolhouse by the flagpole. Many of the parents attended, and after the spelling bee the students who would be going off to high school in the fall recited poems. Then all the pupils were posed for a school photograph.

For once Alvin didn't bother him as they left the schoolyard and walked up the road. Josiah watched Alvin start up the long lane toward the Slade farm. He wouldn't have to see Alvin again for months, not until school started again—that was something to look forward to.

Addy was walking with her mother and little sisters, who had all come for the ceremony. The Pratt boys were running ahead, racing each other. Tom usually won, but not by much. Maybe he'd see them during the summer, even run some races.

As he made his way home by himself that day, Josiah thought about his parents. Ever since coming to the farm, he had tried hard not to think about Ma and Pa, but the sight of all those parents in the schoolyard made him feel empty and lonely all over again.

Then his thoughts turned to Aunt Ethel and Uncle Perry, who had taken him in, and to Uncle Albert, who remained a mystery. He hadn't really found out any more about his uncle or about the dam that everybody talked around.

He did his chores, more or less, but lately he felt he wasn't doing enough to earn his keep, and every day he saw all the work there was to do. Now, with the long summer stretching ahead, he saw a chance to make himself useful, to show them that his pair of hands really could help.

He wondered again if work and chores were why Uncle Albert had left the farm, left the Swift River Valley. Josiah wished he knew how to get Aunt Ethel to tell him more about his uncle. Why hadn't Uncle Albert kept in touch? Why hadn't he written to his sisters? Could a person just disappear, even if he wasn't dead?

6
Finding Bessie

THROUGH SLEEP JOSIAH HEARD THE ROOSTER CROWING. He jumped out of bed, wondering how he could have slept so late again, and dressed hurriedly—he was sure as certain that Uncle Perry and Aunt Ethel were already busy doing chores. He found his aunt in the kitchen, and as he feared, Uncle Perry was already in the barn.

After his trip to the privy, Josiah stopped at the pump, working the handle up and down until cold water came gushing out of the spout. He splashed some at his face and lowered the pump handle carefully. Next he filled two empty pails with water and brought them in for Aunt Ethel. As he put down the pails, she handed him a slab of home-baked bread slathered with butter.

Uncle Perry already had the cows in the tie-up, where they stood waiting to be milked, but he was standing by the ramp at the back of the barn, looking down at the pasture, instead of milking. "Bessie didn't come in with the rest of the cows. I sent Shep to go bring her in, but that fool dog is worse than useless." He looked down at Shep, who thumped his tail at the sound of his name, and he scratched the dog behind the ears. "I'm going to start milking. You go on out and find Bessie."

"Where should I look?" Josiah asked, swallowing the last of his bread and butter.

"Might be down by the brook. Just find her and bring her back."

Josiah nodded. "I'm going," he answered.

Uncle Perry turned toward Daisy's spotted flank, milking stool and pail in hand. Josiah burst out of the dimness of the barn and ran down the back ramp, his eyes surprised by the brightness.

Gray rocks, cow pies, and clumps of manure-fertilized grasses dotted the sloping pasture. Josiah dodged the fresh, gooey pies and hastily stooped to pick a few tiny, wild strawberries, the June sun already hot on his neck. He reached the brook, and still no sign of Bessie. He waded into the stream and felt mud ooze up between his bare toes. The cloven hoofprints that the cattle left when they came to drink were everywhere, but they didn't give him any clue about Bessie. For a moment he watched the clear water of the brook flow around stones, creating bits of foam.

His eyes searched along the brook for Bessie. "Come, Boss. Come, Boss," he called, trying to make his voice sound deep like Uncle Perry's when he called the cows. He'd learned that "Boss," short for "Bossy," was how you called cows if you wanted them to come, or if you didn't know their names. But why, he wondered, were cows called "Bossy" in the first place?

He waded across the brook, slipping on water-smoothed stones, his feet getting numbed by the cold stream. Barbed wire, mostly nailed to trees instead of fence posts, ran along the brook all the way down to the corner by the swamp. He would follow the fence, he decided. In some places the bark of the trees was growing right over the rusting wire. Wherever Bessie was, her milk bag must be getting full and uncomfortable. Cows liked to be milked, if you did it right—that was why they were waiting by the barn door every morning, and Bessie was usually one of the first to come up the ramp.

Almost at the fence corner, his feet sinking into the soft, spongy carpet of moss that grew near the bog, he saw a break in the old, rusted wire. It was plenty big enough for a cow. "Come, Boss. Hey, Bessie," he shouted. Pushing aside a broken strand of barbed wire, he went through the gap in the fence and called again.

"Moooooo!" came an answer from the bog.

Josiah plunged into the shaded swamp, looking in the direction of the moo for the brown-and-white shape of a cow. Now all he had to do was lead her back to the barn for milking. He could already see the smile on Uncle Perry's face, and Uncle Perry didn't smile any too often.

Another long "moooooooooo," but he still couldn't see Bessie. His foot went down, almost to his knee, and if he'd had on shoes, he would have lost the shoe, the way the mud sucked as he pulled out his leg. Mosquitoes buzzed and bit, and the smell of the bog hung in the air. Josiah's foot sank again. About to take another step, he stopped, remembering

Uncle Perry saying to Aunt Ethel, "Only thing that bottomless bog is good for is if you don't want something. Put it in there and it's gone."

At that moment Josiah saw the white patch between Bessie's horns. Her head was low, right near the ground, so she must have fallen, maybe broken her leg. Cautiously, he stepped forward onto squishy hummocks of grass, and then he saw her struggling in a bog hole with no way to climb back out. Only her neck and head were sticking up above the watery surface. The cow gave a bellow of desperation. "Hold on, Bessie, we're coming," he yelled, and then he ran, faster than he ever had, back to the barn, hoping she wouldn't give up and drown before they got back.

Josiah was so out of breath at first that he couldn't make Uncle Perry understand. Aunt Ethel, who was straining milk from the pails into the big milk cans, said, "Whoa down, boy. What do you mean we have to pull her out?"

"Out of the bog! We've got to pull Bessie out of the bog. She's stuck in the bog!"

Aunt Ethel set the milk pail down so fast that milk splashed out onto the floor. "Josiah, get the mare!" Uncle Perry ordered. "I'll get the harness and a whiffletree. Ethel, get us a rope, a long, strong one."

Lead rope in hand, Josiah hesitated outside Big Nellie's stall. He still wasn't comfortable around the tall workhorse. "Over, girl. Over!" he said, hoping the mare would let him into the stall beside her. This time she did. He snapped the lead onto her halter and led her out.

Uncle Perry threw the harness on Big Nellie in no time and hooked the leather traces to the wooden bar of the whiffletree, which kept the traces from tangling and made it easier for her to pull a load. The mare, her hooves larger than saucers, jogged through the pasture toward the swamp, the whiffletree bouncing along behind her. Uncle Perry held on to the long reins; Josiah, panting, ran beside him; and Aunt Ethel, her skirt billowing, brought up the rear. "We can't lose Bessie," she called. "Her milk makes the best butter!"

When the doctor's newfangled automobile had gotten stuck in the spring mud, Josiah had watched as Big Nellie pulled it out easily. Now he wondered how they were going to pull a cow out, but he had more sense than to waste breath on asking Uncle Perry.

Bessie was still thrashing about, unable to find any solid footing. Her eyes rolling wildly, she bellowed and tossed her head. Picking his way carefully from one grass hummock to another, Uncle Perry got as close to the cow as he dared. On the fourth toss, the loop at the end of the long rope settled over her curving horns. Uncle Perry moved back to firmer ground, holding the rope tight.

In a minute he had the rope tied to the ring in the center of the whiffletree. "Now pull, Nellie! Pull!" He slapped the reins on her broad back.

Just as Josiah thought that Bessie's head was going to pull off, the cow began to come out of the deep bog. Nellie moved forward, dragging Bessie by the horns, flat on her side, until the ground was solid. The cow gasped for a bit and then struggled to her feet.

"Lucky thing you have your horns, or we'd never have got you out," Aunt Ethel said, rubbing the white spot on Bessie's face. "It's a good thing that Josiah found you in time," she added, throwing him a smile of thanks. "I wish we didn't have this bog, though."

"Only farm hereabouts with a real bog," Uncle Perry said. "I've thought of draining it, could be done. But if they do flood the valley, this bog will be gone, drowned with everything under all that water."

"So it's true," Josiah exclaimed. "You think they might flood the valley! But I don't understand why."

"We're not talking about that now, about taking our land—not now and not later," Aunt Ethel announced, before her husband could get a word in edgewise. "We need to get this cow up to the barn and see if she has any milk left. I hope she won't go dry."

7
Trip to the Depot

Josiah and uncle perry spent most of the next day fencing, carrying the porcupine-prickly roll of barbed wire between them, each holding the end of a piece of wood thrust through the hole in the center of the roll. After mending the gap that Bessie had made going into the swamp, Uncle Perry stapled up new wire wherever the old was badly rusted. "I don't fix much anymore," he said as he drew a length of wire tight. When it came to replacing a few fence posts, Uncle Perry remarked that he wasn't going to bother using rot-resistant cedar. "No point, not if they're going to take the fences down."

"Who is they, and why would they do that?" Josiah asked, but he didn't get an answer.

They moved to the upper pasture on the hill. Part of the hillside had been logged a number of years back, and blueberries bushes grew in between the tree stumps. Finally they did the fence around the small back pasture, above the main mowing field, where the hay was growing green and tall. They could hear the cows lowing, waiting to be milked.

Soon warm milk hissed into the pail that Josiah held between his knees as he rhythmically squeezed Bessie's teats. He thought back to his first attempt at milking. While he hadn't entirely forgiven Spangle, he guessed he must have looked pretty funny lying in the gutter with his feet up in the air. He finished milking, patted Bessie, and undid the clip on the chain so that she could go back out to the pasture and graze.

That night Aunt Ethel made strawberry shortcake topped with freshly whipped cream for dessert. Josiah had hardly ever eaten strawberries in Boston. "Delicious!" he said as he ate the last bite.

"Don't forget that we have to get an early start tomorrow in the strawberry bed, and then you and Uncle Perry will be going to the depot," Aunt Ethel reminded him.

"Of course I won't forget. I can't wait. I've hardly been back to the depot since I came here," Josiah responded. Usually Uncle Perry went into the village or to Enfield while Josiah was in school, and mostly Aunt Ethel stayed home. She went to church on Sundays, driving old Ned hitched to the buggy, but that was about it. Maybe tomorrow he'd get to see a locomotive up close, maybe the one on the route called the Rabbit Run. That lonely train ride from Boston seemed a long time ago.

The rooster was crowing as Josiah came awake—time to get up and go out to the barn to milk. And right after breakfast, they started picking the strawberries. As Josiah picked, he stopped now and then to jam another juicy berry into his mouth. Soon ripe, red berries were mounded high in dozens and dozens of little baskets.

Big Nellie stood patiently as they loaded the wagon for the trip to the depot. Aunt Ethel handed up a large basket full of extra-big berries. "Don't you eat any of those, Josiah," she said.

"No room. I'm full," he answered, wondering if the basket was a special order. Uncle Perry got up on the wagon box and Josiah climbed up beside him, itching with the excitement of going to town—not that it was much of a town, hardly anything compared to Boston. Anyway, it would be a change. The wagon lurched and swayed as they turned onto the rutted road. Big Nellie jogged and the wagon jostled. They passed the Damon place with its neatly squared stone walls. The oldest Damon girl, Betty, was at the clothesline, hanging out the wash to dry. Josiah looked for Addy, but he didn't see her. He missed their walks to and from school, he realized, and wished he could tell her about finding Bessie in the bog.

They crossed the wooden plank bridge over the brook, each board rattling under Nellie's hooves and the turning wagon wheels. They passed the Pratt farm, with red paint peeling off the old barn and the leaning silo. The lane that led to the Slade farm reminded Josiah of Alvin. "If I never see Alvin again, it will be too soon." He mouthed the words, almost loud enough for Uncle Perry to hear.

The mare kept on jogging and the wagon kept jostling. Finally they came into Enfield and to the depot itself. Josiah looked along the tracks and listened for that long, piercing whistle. "Whoa, Nellie," Uncle Perry said, giving the reins a tug.

Josiah's feet landed in the dust. His shoes, put on for the trip into town, were beginning to pinch. He reached up for a tray of baskets. "What happened?" he asked. "I know there were berries right up over the top of each basket. They were there when we loaded!"

"All shook down," Uncle Perry said, a laugh creeping into his voice. "Your aunt always tells me that they won't sell like this. So she gave us something to fix 'em up." He passed down the basket of extra-large berries. "Put her big beauties right on top in each basket, then we'll get a price that might suit her."

While Uncle Perry took care of selling the berries to be shipped by train, Josiah waited with Nellie. He looked over at a Model T Ford, a Packard, and a touring car parked in front of the hitching posts by the hotel and thought back to streets crowded with honking autos. A man came out of the general store and walked over to him. He scratched his graying hair and put his thumbs behind his overall straps. "You're Ethel's sister's boy, aren't you?"

"Yes, sir."

"From Boston," the man added. "We don't like people from Boston around here."

Josiah looked down at Nellie's hooves.

"The people in Boston want to steal our water, want to dam up the whole dang valley and flood it. That's what they want to do," the man continued.

"I never heard about that in Boston," Josiah said.

"Well, we heard plenty about how the people there are running out of water."

"Not that I ever knew about."

Then Uncle Perry was at Josiah's elbow. "Hiram," he said, "you know it's the politicians in Boston, not the people, who are after our water."

The man let go of his overall straps, and they snapped against his burly chest. "They still want our water," he said, and crossed the street.

Josiah, feeling as if he had suddenly shrunk a size, waited while Uncle Perry went into the store to get sugar and tea for Aunt Ethel. Then he heard the train whistle and saw the locomotive as it came puffing and clanging to a stop at the station platform. He wished he could go look at it close enough to touch instead of staying with the horse. He wished he could board that train and travel along the rails until he got back to Boston.

ONCE THEY WERE OUT OF TOWN, Uncle Perry said, "You take the reins, Josiah," and handed over the long, leather lines. Josiah gave the reins a light slap on the mare's rump, the way Uncle Perry did. Then he made that clucking sound. Nellie swiveled her ears around, raised her head, and broke into a trot.

"Wait a minute, we're not going to the races," Uncle Perry said. Josiah knew his uncle was letting him drive to make up for what that man had said about people from Boston, but he gave the reins another slap, harder this time. Nellie picked up the pace, making the wagon bounce hard over the bumps. Another slap and the wagon nearly careened off the road. "Whoa," he called, pulling back on the reins. As Nellie slowed, Josiah let fly with a question. "If Boston does need more water, why would they come all the way out here looking for it?"

"No point in talking about things you can't do anything about," Uncle Perry answered. While the man named Hiram was more than ready to talk, Aunt Ethel and Uncle Perry seemed bent on avoiding the subject of the dam, as if it were a skunk about to spray.

When they came to the bridge over the brook, Josiah looked down at the clear, rushing stream and tried to imagine that water going all the way to the city of Boston. It wasn't like sending strawberries on the train. It didn't seem right. It didn't even seem possible.

8

Wind Storm

It had been a sunny week, with only a few fluffy clouds that looked like flocks of sheep being herded across the blueness of the sky, and not a drop of rain. Uncle Perry had been pushing all week to finish with the haying. First there was the cutting, with the sickle-bar mower clattering behind Big Nellie; next came the big, curving, horse-drawn rake moving the dried grass into windrows; and then they pitched the hay onto the wagon, although Josiah couldn't pitch very high. Mr. Damon had come one day to help. Now they were bringing in the last wagonload, with Josiah perched on top of the mound of hay as the mare pulled the swaying hayrack to the barn.

After Uncle Perry had forked the last wisps of hay up into the loft, they still had the milking to do. But first Josiah went to the pump, cupped his hands and drank, and then lifted the bucket and poured all the rest of the water over his head, washing off the sweat of the day's haying and the bits of hay that stuck to his face and bare, sunburned back.

By the time they came into the kitchen after milking, Josiah thought that all he wanted to do was sleep, but that was before he smelled Aunt Ethel's strawberry rhubarb pie.

The next morning, Josiah came awake still feeling stiff all over. He propped his head up on his elbow. The sun was already over the horizon, slanting through the small panes of the window by his bed. He was late. But maybe, just maybe, he thought, I can go to the swimming hole in the brook today and practice. He'd gone once with the Pratt boys; it wasn't far from the schoolhouse.

"Can you swim? Dog-paddle, at least?" he remembered Addy asking him.

"Not very well," he'd answered, thinking of the few times Ma and Pa had taken him to a pond near Boston. Mostly he'd just splashed and waded.

"Almost all the boys here swim some," she'd told him.

So it would be fun to try swimming, unless Alvin was there. He'd heard Alvin boast about how he could dive. If Alvin was there, it wouldn't be fun at all.

Uncle Perry's voice came up the farmhouse stairs. "Day's a-wasting! We've got to go help Mr. Damon with his haying. The weather's not going to hold."

Josiah sighed, pulled on his clothes, and headed for the outhouse. The stench was pretty bad because of the summer heat. He held his breath and tried not to breathe at all, his lungs almost bursting before he was through. No wonder people wanted indoor plumbing, with flush toilets and water coming out of faucets. Of course, he realized, then they would use more water, not like pumping it by hand up out of the well. A city like Boston must use a lot of water.

As soon as the milking was finished, they went into the kitchen for breakfast. Josiah ate an egg, biscuits, and the last slice of the strawberry rhubarb pie. Uncle Perry polished off three eggs, bacon, and biscuits. Soon they were striding down the road to the Damon place, pitchforks and a rake in hand. Maybe at least I'll see Addy, Josiah thought.

It was a boy's job, his job for today, to "rake after," using the long-handled hay rake with its straight wooden tines to gather any hay left behind as the men "pitched on" and made the load. They worked together as clouds gathered in the northwest.

There were distant rumbles of thunder. "It'll blow over," Mr. Damon said, looking at the hay that still lay in the field. The sky darkened, thunder rolled, a drop of rain fell. Then the sky cleared and the sun beat down on them again.

Another load into the Damons' big barn. Josiah rested for a moment, leaning on the rake, and his eyes swept over the hay field and then the upper pasture where the cows that would munch hay all winter now grazed on grass. Beyond them was the woodlot, rising into forested hills, and above everything the sky. They all looked at the sky. "Light's odd," Uncle Perry said. "We're in for it this time, Fred."

"Naw," responded Mr. Damon, "we'll make it with the last loads." Black clouds mounted and wind began stirring the tops of the trees. The sky growled ominously. Just after they started back to the hay field, they heard the coming of the rain, a heavy patter rushing down the hill. Drops as big as blueberries pelted them and drenched the hay waiting in the field.

Soaked, they took cover in the large woodshed near the house. Rain and then hail rattled on the tin roof, as if the sky were shooting nails. Lightning split the clouds; thunder boomed and cracked. Wind came in fierce gusts. A branch was torn off the maple tree in front of the house and dashed to the ground. Josiah stood looking out through the sheets of rain toward the barn with its big, wide-open doors. An enormous billow of wind roared over the shed and right in through the barn doors. The roof of the barn lifted, seemed to be suspended in the air, then crashed down lopsided onto the back wall, shingles flying off every which way. Rain poured down. Josiah's jaw dropped open.

"Oh my God, the roof's gone!" Mr. Damon yelled. "Oh my God," he said again, softly this time, as if he couldn't believe his own eyes. The roof wasn't exactly gone, Josiah thought, but it sat crazily, the beams of the old barn bending and creaking beneath the unbalanced weight. For an instant Josiah was reminded of old Mrs. Glover back in Boston, who put her hats on sideways and backwards, only this wasn't funny.

Some of the siding gave way, and a shower of roof shingles tumbled down into the barnyard. The men stood there, staring, quiet except for the drumming of rain on the roof. Then Mr. Damon said, "Don't guess we're going to get that hay into the barn after all. Might as well call it a day."

"I never imagined seeing such a thing," Uncle Perry said. "I suppose all that air went in the big doorway and there was nowhere for it to go but up. Too bad you didn't have the back doors open." He shook his head.

Josiah found that he was shaking with the unexpectedness of it. You couldn't count on things staying the same—the top could blow off, the bottom drop out.

"We could all get together and fix it. Put a new roof on for you, Fred," Uncle Perry suggested to Mr. Damon. "Like an old-time barn raising."

"Not worth it, not the way things are," Mr. Damon replied, looking at the ground instead of at his ruined barn.

Josiah was wondering why it wouldn't be worth it, when Mr. Damon pulled himself together and explained stiffly, "I appreciate the offer, but we all know that the handwriting is on the wall. There's no stopping them taking all our barns and flooding this valley. No point in putting on a new roof."

"But what will you do?" Uncle Perry asked.

"I'll have to talk with Ida. Maybe it's time for us to go, before they force us out. And even if they don't dam the river, there are all those new state regulations coming—how many windows in your barn, no manure pile under the barn, tuberculosis tests for all the cows, whitewash everything. Boston wants to control everything, it seems. Might be better in another state."

Josiah could see Mrs. Damon standing at the kitchen door, clutching the baby. Addy came running through the rain to the shed. She stood, looking up at her father, water dripping from the ends of her braids. "Oh, Pa. Pa, the roof is all broken!" she exclaimed.

Mr. Damon just shook his head.

BY THE TIME JOSIAH AND UNCLE PERRY WERE WALKING HOME, the sun was out again and the breeze hardly moved a leaf. Josiah's head was full of questions, but Uncle Perry's face was grim, his mouth as if it were sewn shut, straight across.

After they told her what had happened, Aunt Ethel asked plenty of questions, but not the ones that Josiah wanted answered. She asked, "Do you think they'd go to Ida's folks out in Ohio? Or maybe to Fred's brother up in New Hampshire? That's not so far to go, but Ida's not keen on it. How can they sell the place, though? What could they get for it now?"

"Fred didn't really say" was all the answer she got, tension sizzling beneath the words. And then Uncle Perry said that it was time to milk and that the boy had better go let the cows into the tie-up.

Later, after supper, when Aunt Ethel was doing the washing up and Josiah was drying the dishes for her, he asked, "What handwriting did Mr. Damon mean on which wall? He said that the handwriting was on the wall."

She wiped her hands on her apron and turned away from the dishpan. "For Heaven's sake, boy. That's from the Good Book, from the Bible. It means you've been told, warned what's coming, what's going to happen."

"But what *is* going to happen?" Josiah asked. She turned back to the dishpan and didn't answer.

Josiah jammed his hands into his pockets, pushing down his impatience.

9

The Icehouse, the Fourth of July, and Ice Cream

JOSIAH REACHED ACROSS THE BREAKFAST TABLE for another piece of hot cornbread as Aunt Ethel said, "They'll be having the Independence Day parade in Enfield next week, so I heard."

A parade, Josiah thought. There would be marching bands, columns of soldiers wearing uniforms, prancing horses, fire engines, and flags flying. He smiled as he spread butter on his cornbread, thinking of how the crowd would cheer. Maybe there would even be fireworks. He could hardly wait.

"I don't think we'll go this year," Uncle Perry said. "Fred Damon told me they're not going—nothing to celebrate in this valley."

The words sank in and Josiah stopped chewing. No parade. Slowly he finished his cornbread, pushed back his chair, and carried his plate over to the soapstone sink under the window. He stood there, looking out at the garden, the fields and hills. His parents had taken him to a parade in Boston once. It was when he was still so little that he sat on his father's shoulders, high above the crowd. He remembered looking out over everybody's hats and the excitement of the band music.

Aunt Ethel brought the rest of the dishes to the sink. "I'll get these washed up," she said, and put a hand on Josiah's shoulder. She looked over at Uncle Perry. "If the Damons aren't going," she said, "then why don't we ask them to come here and we'll make ice cream? I think Ida and the girls might like that."

"Might," Uncle Perry answered, with a shrug. "The garden needs hoeing," he added, looking at Josiah, "and I've got to mend Nellie's harness."

HOEING. HE DIDN'T FEEL LIKE HOEING JUST NOW—another chore to help earn his keep. There was always something that needed to be done on a farm. You had to take care of the animals and the vegetables and the crops and even the trees. There was no end to it. That had to be why Uncle Albert left, because he was sick of all the work. Josiah wondered what Uncle Albert was doing now, if he was alive or dead.

Still thinking about the uncle he had never met, Josiah went to the barn, got the hoe, shouldered it, and walked over to the big vegetable garden. Peas climbed the garden fence, their tendrils clinging and their fat, bumpy pods dangling. Rows of radishes, carrots, parsnips, and spinach were followed by rows of bush beans, lettuce, beets, cucumbers, squash, tomatoes, parsley, and cabbage. There were also potatoes, onions, pole beans, and sweet corn.

Last week he had made the mistake of saying to Uncle Perry that there weren't enough weeds to make it worth hoeing. "The whole idea is that you hoe before the weeds take over, not after," Uncle Perry had exploded. Now Josiah whacked the hoe under the few weeds that had dared to come up since he'd last hoed. After whacking his way down one row and up the next, he felt much better.

A garden was full of surprises—green things sprouting up and growing, changing from one day to the next. There was also order in a garden, each plant where it was supposed to be, and he liked that. As he worked, Josiah thought about the parade in Enfield that he wouldn't get to see, and about the Damons and their ruined barn.

Once the hoeing was done, he started picking peas into the rectangular splint basket Aunt Ethel had handed him as he went out the screen door. The bumpy pods were warm from the sun. He pressed one open, poured out peas, and tasted their fresh, sweet flavor. He opened another pod, six peas this time, and that made him think of the Damons again. If they came on Independence Day, he would be surrounded by girls, six of them like the six peas in the pod. There was one bumpy pea in this pod, not round and smooth like the rest. He decided that one must be Addy, with her wild ideas and her curiosity.

Still, they were all girls; even the baby was a girl. Everybody said it must be hard for them having no boys to help with the farmwork, and all those girls to dress and marry. Aunt Ethel said they would "daughter out," with no one left to carry on the family name.

On the morning of the Fourth, Aunt Ethel got down on her hands and knees and poked her head into the pantry cupboard. She brought out a wooden bucket with some odd metal pieces inside.

"What's that thing for?" Josiah asked.

"It's the ice-cream maker! We'd better soak the bucket for a bit so it will swell up and won't leak. It can soak while I make the custard and scald out the can and dasher. We haven't used it for years, just the two of us," she said. "Now, Josiah, get me some more kindling for the stove."

He filled the woodbox next to the hot, black cookstove for the second time that morning. Aunt Ethel brushed perspiration from her forehead with a corner of her apron. "Now then, you go along and help Uncle Perry set up some sawhorses and boards for a table underneath the big maple. Then bring in rock salt and the ice, enough ice for the icebox as well as the ice cream."

The icehouse was one of Josiah's favorite places on the farm, at least on a hot day. Uncle Perry had explained how big blocks of ice were cut from a nearby pond in winter, then hauled home to the farm on a sled. Piled up in the icehouse, they were covered with sawdust from the village sawmill. The sawdust insulated the ice and absorbed water as the blocks began to melt. The icehouse, set against the north side of the barn, was always cool. Uncle Perry took big, curving tongs and lifted a heavy chunk of ice onto the wooden wheelbarrow. Josiah brushed off damp sawdust and wheeled the barrow over to the pump, where he washed off the remaining sawdust, revealing a great, gleaming, glistening cube.

Then Uncle Perry went to work with the sharp ice pick, breaking off small pieces of ice to use in the ice-cream maker. Josiah picked up a piece, sucked on it, and collected the rest in pails. Uncle Perry finished with the ice pick, drying it on his shirttail. "You could kill someone with this," he said, stabbing the pick into the air. "A man in Greenwich threatened to take an ice pick to the next Boston surveyor he saw on his land." Josiah imagined the sharp point of an ice pick sliding between ribs.

Aunt Ethel poured the custard into the ice-cream maker's can and set the dasher in the middle of the can, where it would stir the custard when someone turned the crank on the side of the bucket. Then she filled the space between the can and the sides of the wooden bucket with the ice pieces and rock salt. The Damon family arrived just as they were ready to crank the ice cream. Betty, being the oldest girl, went to help the women and mind the baby while the three little girls got to turn the crank. Addy and Josiah watched the little ones take turns. Addy explained that the cranking was still easy because the ice cream hadn't started to freeze yet. Then Addy cranked until her arms strained to get the crank around. Finally she puffed and gave the job over to Josiah. Uncle Perry added more ice and salt to the freezer bucket. Josiah cranked as the custard inside the can finished freezing, hoping Addy would notice how his new muscles bulged. Finally Aunt Ethel pronounced the ice cream "done," took out the dasher, and said all the girls should have a lick, smallest first, Addy last. Josiah watched Addy's tongue polish the dasher clean.

"Bet you had ice cream every day in Boston," she said.

"No, hardly ever," Josiah answered, "but I wish I had, and this is the first time I ever helped make it."

"Oh," she said, "but you had electricity and electric lights, I bet—and an automobile?"

"We had electricity, of course, but no automobile. There are lots of trolleys and streetcars in Boston. Besides, we couldn't afford an auto."

"Did you have a good well?" she asked. "We have a well right inside our house."

"No, no well."

"Where did your water come from, then? Was there a brook?"

Josiah almost laughed. "The water came out of the faucets," he answered.

Addy stamped her foot and threw back her head, tossing her long braids. "You had indoor plumbing! I thought only rich people had that. Were you rich, even if you didn't have an auto?

"No, we weren't rich," Josiah answered. "Not at all."

"The Pratts have 'gravity feed' from a spring up the hill—the pipe comes down right into their kitchen," Addy went on. "Was it like that? Where did your water come from before it came out of the faucets?"

"I don't know. Never thought about it," Josiah replied.

"How could you not think about your water? What if it went dry?"

"In Boston the water doesn't go dry. I just don't know where they get it." Josiah's face colored. Why did the girl always have to ask so many questions?

"I know where your water came from," Mr. Damon announced. Josiah's face got redder; he hadn't known the man was listening. "It came from the Wachusett Reservoir. That's about thirty miles east of here, going toward Boston. Way back in 1895 the City of Boston took that land and built a reservoir. Then they put in a big pipe to carry the water to Boston—that's about thirty miles of pipe, I guess. Some of the people whose land they took moved here. Now Boston says it needs more water, and so they want to dam our Swift River." He shook his head.

Josiah moved away, before Addy could ask more questions, before he could hear any more about Boston wanting water. He saw Aunt Ethel scooping ice cream into little dishes and putting raspberries on top, but suddenly he didn't care about tasting it. Why hadn't he asked Mr. Damon about Boston needing water? Was he getting like Aunt Ethel, not wanting to talk about things, to face the possibilities?

10
Raspberries, Blueberries, and Fish

Josiah found that these days he was always hungry for breakfast. Now there was only one last spoonful of raspberries left at the bottom of his bowl—the berries like shimmering red islands set in a lake of cream. Josiah captured the islands with his spoon and picked up the bowl to finish the cream. He saw Aunt Ethel watching him and knew that his ma would have told him that drinking out of his bowl was bad manners. He started to put the bowl down.

"Go ahead, drink the cream—don't waste it! I'll look the other way," Aunt Ethel told him, her eyebrows rising. "I don't suppose you ever picked a raspberry," she remarked as he put the empty bowl down.

"Haven't," Josiah admitted, wondering what difference it made. Aunt Ethel had been coming in from the raspberry patch with baskets of delicious berries for the last week.

"The berries are getting ahead of me," she admitted. "They're too fragile to ship, so I'll make jam. If you could go pick while I get the jars and everything ready, well, that would be a help."

"I'll pick for you," he replied, feeling guilty that he hadn't thought to offer to help. Taking the baskets, he went out. The raspberry patch, made up of several long rows of the tall raspberry stems, called canes, was set to the side of the kitchen garden. The berries glinted like jewels—like rubies, he thought—in the sunlight. Josiah plucked off a few raspberries. They almost fell into his hand, and he sampled their sweetness. As he filled the baskets, he imagined how ripe raspberries would jostle down to nothing before they got to the depot, never mind getting to Springfield or Worcester or Boston.

Even before he opened the screen door into the kitchen, Josiah felt the heat from the wood-burning stove. It was hotter inside than being in the sun outside, and Aunt Ethel was mopping her face with a corner of her apron.

"Bring them on over here," she said. He watched her measure berries and sugar and put the deep pot on the stove to boil. She wiped her forehead again, reminding Josiah of something his mother used to say: "Horses sweat, men perspire, and ladies get all of a glow." Well, Aunt Ethel was glowing as bright as a lantern!

"It's hot work, canning in summer. Makes me drip," she said, as if she knew his thoughts. "But that's when it has to be done, so nothing will go to waste and so we'll have them for the winter."

She hates to waste anything, Josiah thought. I wish I had a penny for every time she says, "Waste not, want not." Then I'd be rich, but she'd still say not to waste. That lesson, he thought, seems to be right at the bottom of everything.

A WEEK OR SO LATER, IT WAS BLUEBERRIES. One morning Josiah came in from taking slops out to the pigs, and Aunt Ethel gave him two tin pails and pointed him up the hill. He was already among the scattered high-bush blueberries when he saw someone—a girl with long reddish braids. It could only be Addy Damon.

"What are you doing up here in our back pasture?"

"Same as you," Addy answered. "Picking blueberries. Last summer your aunt told me I could pick all I wanted. She said she only has two hands and she couldn't begin to pick them all. And that if I didn't get them, then the birds would. Of course," Addy added with a laugh, pointing to the greedy blue jays and robins squawking in the bushes, "the birds get more than we do anyway."

Josiah saw that Addy already had one big pail full to the brim. "Is your ma going to can them?" he asked.

"Actually, I'm picking them for my clothes," Addy responded.

"What do you mean?"

"Sometimes you don't understand anything, do you?" She shrugged her shoulders. "I'll need new clothes come fall and school again. Ma said if I pick berries we can sell them in town to the summer people, or make jam and sell that. Then there'll be a bit of money to buy some material to sew new clothes, a dress or something." She explained it all as if she were talking to one of her little sisters.

Josiah shrugged, and they both went to picking. His pail was a quarter full when Addy said, "Did you hear that more people are giving up and moving out of Prescott? There's going to be an auction of their things next week. If we move, I'd hate to watch our things get auctioned."

Josiah didn't say anything, but it made him think of his ma's rocker and how he couldn't leave it. He started picking on a big bush. The berries were hanging thick in clusters, so he could strip them off, almost like milking. He tasted a few berries, to make sure they were as good as they looked. "Addy, there's lots over here," he called.

She came over, her second pail nearly full. "We might move at the end of the summer," she announced.

"I guess your pa really isn't going to fix the barn, then."

"He would if he didn't think we'll all have to leave anyhow, because they'll dam up the whole valley. He says the Swift River Valley is doomed." Addy looked over at the hills and down across the fields to the brook. "I can't imagine this all full of water," she said.

"Can't," Josiah agreed. But somehow he couldn't ask her about the "doom." He guessed he was beginning to understand why Aunt Ethel wouldn't talk—it was a way to make something go away. He went on picking for a bit, trying not to think about Boston wanting water.

"My sister Betty, she can't wait to leave. She wants us to move to where she can go to the moving pictures every week, where she can get a factory job and have indoor plumbing. You must have seen a lot of picture shows before you came here."

"No, my parents didn't let me go. Well, I went once with a friend."

"Was it real exciting, the way they say it is?" Addy wanted to know.

"Not the one I saw. It was kind of silly."

"Oh," said Addy, and Josiah saw that she looked disappointed.

"My pails are full, and I better get on home," she said, and started to leave. But she turned back and asked him, "Do you ever go fishing?"

"Never have," Josiah answered, thinking it was a funny question for a girl to ask, but with Addy you never knew what was next.

"I'm going fishing tomorrow morning after chores, if you want to come." She stood there holding the heavy pails of berries. "I can wait for you by the bridge."

"Maybe I can. I'll have to ask my aunt."

Addy turned again and started toward the Damon farm, walking slowly so as not to spill the berries.

Coming down the hill, Josiah was not so careful—his thoughts were switching like trains in a yard between water for Boston, people leaving, and going fishing. He spilled some berries and hoped that Aunt Ethel wouldn't scold because one pail wasn't quite full anymore.

"Well now," she exclaimed. "That's enough for at least two pies, jam, and some blueberry muffins besides. Picked nice and clean, too, no stems or sticks or leaves that I can see. Your ma picked her berries like that, but my brother Albert . . ." She stopped and shook her head. "He didn't like picking, only eating. There were always leaves and twigs in his pail." Aunt Ethel took the blueberries and gave Josiah a big smile.

Josiah couldn't help but bask for a moment in the warmth of that smile. Then he decided that, before he could change his mind, he would ask about tomorrow. "Addy Damon was up there picking. She picks faster than I can, and she wants to know if I can go fishing tomorrow. Can I?"

"Fishing? Fishing with Addy Damon?" The surprise came and went across her face. "Well, I guess it wouldn't do you any harm, once the chores are done. If you catch some brookies, I'll fry them up for supper. Uncle Perry never was much for fishing. Now, you come on out to the woodshed, and we'll see if Albert's old pole is still hanging up where it's been all these years since he left."

THE NEXT MORNING, JOSIAH HURRIED DOWN THE ROAD with the long fishing pole over his shoulder. He thought that Addy might not have waited, as Uncle Perry had made him hill up some of the potatoes after his regular chores, burying them deeper so they wouldn't turn green. But as he came around the corner, his feet kicking up dust in the road, he saw her sitting on a rock below the bridge, her toes in the water.

"Where'd you get that rod?" was the first thing she said.

"It once belonged to my Uncle Albert," he answered.

"My pa told me that he used to fish with your uncle when they were boys, right in this brook. He said that Albert was a real rascal, too."

"What did he do?"

"Pa didn't tell me. Wish I had a rod like that, a store-bought rod. I brought some extra worms and a few tied flies for bait."

"How come you know how to fish? My Aunt Ethel told me that only boys got to go fishing when she was a girl."

Addy flung her head, making her braids flap on her back. "It's because we don't have any boys. Betty would never think of fishing. She's even afraid of worms. But Pa, he loves to angle. He says we have some of the best streams in the whole world for brook trout right here in the Swift River Valley. Well, I asked him if I could learn to fish, even though I'm a girl, so he taught me how."

They walked a ways downstream to where trees partly shaded the brook. Clear water rushed along between rocks, making small waterfalls and creating a music of its own. Sometime, he thought, I'll come back here with my notebook and try to draw a waterfall.

Addy stopped where the stream widened and the water slowed. "We'll start with worms," she said. "That's easier than casting out with flies." She showed Josiah how to put a worm onto the hook and then toss it out into the middle of the pool. After she made a few tosses, Josiah saw her line jerk, and before he could tell how, she was holding a fish in her hands, getting the hook out of its mouth and putting it into a basket.

Again Josiah tossed out his line, and suddenly there was a strong tug, making the reel by the handle of his rod spin.

"You've got one! Pull it in. Pull it in!" Addy yelled.

He grabbed at the reel and finally got it winding in. Then the fish pulled away again.

"Play him. Play him!" Addy instructed, whatever that meant. The fish jumped out of the water, and he could see that it was a big one, much bigger than Addy's.

The trout tugged hard and the reel whipped around before Josiah got the fish coming toward him once more. Wouldn't Aunt Ethel be pleased with such a big fish! He felt proud already.

"Now you have to land him," Addy exclaimed. "Bring him in!"

Josiah gave a hard pull, and suddenly there was nothing. No fish.

"You lost him," Addy announced, as if he couldn't see that for himself. As if he didn't know how quickly things could be lost, taken away.

11
Eggs

THREE SMALL BROOK TROUT SIZZLED IN THE CAST-IRON FRYING PAN and then were on three plates, along with new potatoes and green beans from the garden. For several minutes nobody said anything while they all ate. After the first few delicious bites, Josiah wanted to tell them about the big fish, but Addy had warned him not to. "They never believe you when you tell them about the ones that get away," she said.

"These brookies are a tasty change," Aunt Ethel commented, finishing her fish. "You can't get fresh fish here unless you catch it, not like Boston where you're by the ocean."

"Lots of streams in this valley," Uncle Perry added. "People come from all over to fish here—spend the day getting their feet wet and throwing a long bit of string into the water. Of course, if this valley became one great big lake, it would have bigger fish, I suppose." He looked over at Aunt Ethel, but her lips were set into that firm line. Nobody said anything more.

THE NEXT MORNING, JOSIAH WENT TO THE CHICKEN HOUSE AS USUAL to collect the eggs. He looked first to see if Rufus, the big rooster, was strutting about in the yard. Rufus, with his beady eyes and sharp talons, had attacked Josiah's trousers more than once. Pecking hens were bad enough, but Rufus really made him nervous. Once he'd seen Shep come too close to one of the hens, and the rooster had jumped right onto the dog's back, pecking at his ears and drawing blood. Shep had run off with his tail between his legs, and Josiah didn't blame him one bit.

Having located Rufus out in the yard, Josiah went into the chicken house. A few hens were scratching around or getting a drink from the waterer. The broody hen was still sitting in her box. Josiah knew there were twelve eggs under her soft, warm breast feathers, so that would be a dozen more chicks when they hatched. Except that Aunt Ethel would say, "Never count your chickens before they hatch." She was probably right, as usual. The last broody hen, that big speckled one, had sat on fourteen eggs and only six had hatched.

The nest boxes, where the hens were meant to lay their eggs, were nailed up on one wall. A hen hopped out of a box. "Kut-kut, kut, kuda-ket!" she crowed, proclaiming, " I've laid an egg, I've laid an egg!" Josiah took the brown egg from the box and held it for a moment in his hand before adding it to the others in the basket. It was still warm from the body of the hen, and it seemed strange and miraculous that such a thing could hatch into a chick, all ready to peck and scratch about. This made him think of the old question they asked each other on the playground of his school in Boston: which came first, the chicken or the egg? Now he knew a lot about chickens and eggs, but he still didn't know the answer. He laughed out loud at himself.

Perhaps surprised by his laugh, a hen fluttered down from her perch on a narrow beam that ran above the roosting poles. Josiah glanced up at the beam and saw an egg sitting there, balancing. Sometimes hens laid eggs in odd places, but he didn't usually look up at the beam. He supposed he would have to figure out how to get this one down. He considered getting a ladder to reach the egg, but he decided that he could just climb up on the roosts and grab it.

Josiah's feet balanced on a round roosting pole while one hand grasped the beam and the other inched toward the egg. Just a little more and he would close his hand carefully around that egg. But his feet slipped, his fingers knocked the egg off the beam, and as he fell he was enveloped by a nauseating, choking odor. The egg! Worse, the shattered, stinking egg was smashed underneath him, and his foot kicked over the basket of good eggs, breaking several. With all the commotion, the broody hen jumped off her nest and ran out the small chicken door, clucking loudly.

Attempting not to breathe because of the stink, Josiah picked himself up and stood for a moment, deciding what to do next. He'd have to go tell Aunt Ethel about the egg. He put the unbroken eggs back in the basket and went up to the house. Aunt Ethel must have smelled him before she saw him. She hollered through the screen door, "Don't you dare come in here smelling like that! Don't you have more sense than to break rotten eggs?"

"But I didn't know it was rotten! It was up on the beam and it looked like any other egg, and now it's burst."

"I can tell that; you smell worse than skunk on a dog. Be glad it doesn't cling as long as skunk. Now, you go back to that chicken house with a shovel and the wheelbarrow. Clean up all the floor litter that got egg on it and take the whole mess out to the manure pile and bury it. Then fill that old washtub with water and put your clothes in the tub before you scrub yourself off under the pump. I'll bring out a towel and soap. And," she added, "I promise I won't look."

Josiah did as he was told, but suddenly what he wanted more than anything was a real bathroom with a big, smooth, slippery bathtub filled with suds and hot water that ran out of a faucet. He was tired of trying to fit in on a farm—like a square peg being pounded into a round hole. No matter how hard he tried, it seemed that it wasn't enough.

After Josiah washed, scrubbed, and dried off, he wrapped the towel around his middle and went in to put on some clean clothes. He sat on the bed and thought of Uncle Albert leaving the farm, going west, away from all this. Finally he went back down the stairs, hoping to slip out past his aunt.

"Wait a minute," she called, and sat him down at the kitchen table. "I shouldn't have snapped at you," she said. "That smell made me think of years ago when Albert tossed a rotten egg to me and told me to catch. It broke all over my hands. Heaven only knows when this egg was laid. But it's a lucky, lucky thing for me that you broke it."

"What do you mean, lucky?" Josiah asked in surprise.

"Well, if you'd brought it in whole, and I'd gone to fry it up for Uncle Perry's breakfast, then it would have exploded at me and all over my kitchen! So I ought to thank you." Then she gave him one of her smiles, and a piece of blueberry pie.

12
Achilles and Alvin

A FEW DAYS LATER, JOSIAH WAS PUTTING SLOPS INTO THE TROUGH for the pigs when Uncle Perry came and stood behind him. "Pigs are filling out good, beginning to put on some weight," he said. "But don't you pay too much attention to them, or else the bacon won't taste right. When I was a boy, over in Erving where I grew up, they gave me a little runt pig to raise on a bottle. In the fall we butchered my pig, but I never could eat any of it." Uncle Perry turned away as if he still missed that pig.

He's right, Josiah thought. If you don't care about something, then it doesn't matter what happens to it. It can't hurt you if you don't care.

The next morning, after milking, Uncle Perry let all the cows back out to pasture except for Buttercup. "You know where the Slade place is, don't you?" he asked Josiah.

"Yes," Josiah answered. He could see himself walking back from the schoolhouse, and he could see Alvin Slade turning off and going up to his big farm. Would Alvin still make fun of him and call him "Boston Boy" when school started again?

"Buttercup is ready to be serviced. So you can lead her on over there after chores."

"Do I have to?" Josiah asked, then wished that he had never let the words out of his mouth. It was all because he didn't want to see Alvin.

Uncle Perry gave him a funny look but didn't answer. So Josiah asked another question, hoping Uncle Perry would forget the first one. "What kind of service does she need?"

Uncle Perry laughed. "I can tell you didn't start on a farm." Then he hesitated, as if he wasn't sure what to say next. "They have a bull, and otherwise, she won't have a calf. That's all."

Then Josiah felt foolish—of course, it was all about mating. He could tell that his face was getting red.

Uncle Perry didn't seem to notice.

On the way to the Slade farm, Josiah let Buttercup stop to eat grass by the side of the dusty road whenever she wanted. He was in no hurry. When they passed the Damon farm, he hoped he might see Addy, but he didn't. Maybe, if he could think of an excuse, he would stop there on his way back.

As they went over the bridge, he looked down at the brook. It was August now and there was much less water than there had been when school let out; it had even gone down some since he went fishing with Addy. Finally they turned off and started up the long drive to the Slade place. He noticed that the house had a fresh coat of white paint on it and the barn had new windows. Josiah pulled on Buttercup's lead rope and looked around, hoping not to see Alvin. Mr. Slade came out of the house. He looked like a taller, beefier version of Alvin. They both had thick necks and small, blue eyes.

Taking Buttercup's lead rope, Mr. Slade said, "You tell your uncle I'll take care of his cow, or, rather, that Achilles will. Achilles is a fine bull. You see him over there?" The bull, catching sight, or was it scent, of a new cow, came trotting toward them, head and horns high. Josiah noticed that the fence around his small pasture was reinforced everywhere. Achilles snorted and pawed, his nose ring tossing up and down. Buttercup backed away, pulling on the lead rope. Josiah guessed that she didn't like the idea of being left with Achilles. He was glad that Uncle Perry didn't keep a bull.

"I'll be going now," Josiah said to Mr. Slade. But just then Alvin came out of the barn, holding an old hen by the legs. He came right over to Josiah and said, "I want to show you something, something I bet a Boston boy has never seen." Josiah didn't know why, but he followed Alvin around behind the barn.

"Now we're going to have some fun," Alvin announced.

They were standing near a large chopping block made from a piece of a tree trunk. Next to the block Josiah saw a heavy cleaver lying on the ground. The hen squawked as Alvin laid her down on top of the block, one hand holding her firmly. As soon as the chicken was still, Alvin picked up the cleaver and whacked it down onto the hen's head, right behind the eyes.

Then Alvin put the hen down on the ground and let go of her legs. The headless hen, blood spurting out of her neck, ran around and around.

"Can't you stop it!" Josiah demanded.

"Why should I want to stop it?" Alvin laughed. "I didn't think a Boston boy ever saw a chicken running around with its head cut off. Guess I was right!" he gloated.

Josiah turned away, his stomach churning, and started the long walk home.

"See you when school starts, Boston Boy," Alvin called after him.

13
Sharpening

Josiah brought a bushel basket of tomatoes into the kitchen and set it down on the wide-plank floor. He saw the canning kettle, the glass jars, lids, and rubber rings all set out on the table, but Aunt Ethel wasn't there. The morning sun was streaming in through the small-paned parlor windows, and he spotted her sitting by the desk with a box in her lap. A desk drawer stood open, and she was reading an article cut out of a newspaper.

"I brought in the tomatoes for you," he announced, standing in the doorway. He saw her start at the sound of his voice, but she didn't get up. "I'm sorry if I interrupted your reading," he said, wondering what could make his normally busy aunt sit so still.

"I'll put this away," she said, hurriedly folding up the clipping. "It's just an article about damming the river, from a Boston newspaper. A friend sent it to Mrs. Pratt, and she gave it to me on Sunday after church. So I'm saving it."

Josiah knew that Aunt Ethel liked to save everything. "You can never tell when something could come in handy. We might need it, find a use for it," she would remark, but this was different.

"What does the article say? Will you tell me?" Josiah asked.

"Same old thing," she answered, shaking her head. She looked into the box and sorted slowly through a pile of clippings. At last she looked up, a clipping in her hand. "Here's one I can show you. It's a poem written in 1921 by a man from Prescott. They published it in the *Athol Transcript*."

Josiah came across the room and took the piece of yellowed newspaper from her. Silently, he read:

> *Prescott is my home, though*
> *rough and poor she be.*
>
> *The home of many a noble soul,*
> *the birthplace of the free.*
>
> *I love her rock-bound woods and hills,*
> *they are good enough for me.*
>
> *I love her brooklets and her rills,*
> *but couldn't, wouldn't, and*
> *shouldn't love a man-made sea.*

He read it a second time, at first not understanding what the poet meant by a man-made sea, and then he realized that, of course, the poem was about what would happen if they dammed up the river, about what would be lost. He looked over at Aunt Ethel and swallowed hard. "Addy Damon told me that people are leaving Prescott. They're auctioning off their things."

"They're tired of waiting, waiting to see when, or if, the ax will fall," she responded. "But I don't like to talk about it, and besides, I can't believe that the water would ever come this high, to our farm," she added, holding out her hand for the clipping. She tucked it carefully into the box, put the box into the drawer, and quickly closed the drawer. Getting up from the chair, she said, more to herself than to Josiah, "I'd best get to work on those tomatoes. I believe there's time to scald them, skin them, boil them up, put them into jars, and get them into the canning kettle before dinner."

All that work, Josiah thought. All that work so we can have stewed tomatoes to eat over the winter. And I don't even like stewed tomatoes. He stood there for a moment, watching his aunt bustle about the kitchen and wondering if the man who wrote the poem about Prescott still lived there. He wanted to ask Aunt Ethel, but while he hesitated she gave him the look with her eyebrows pulled together and said, "You go along out and find Uncle Perry. Find something useful to do."

As Josiah walked toward the barn, he considered whether it might be "useful" to go fishing. He'd tried it a couple of times since the day he went with Addy, but he hadn't caught a thing. Shep came running to him, tail wagging, and Josiah rubbed the dog behind the ears.

He found Uncle Perry sharpening a scythe on the old grindstone. Uncle Perry's foot pressed rhythmically on the wooden pedal-board attached to the crank on the stone wheel. Josiah watched the heavy wheel turn, dipping down into the water trough set beneath it and then up to where Uncle Perry held the blade at an angle to the stone. Josiah's eyes went round and round with the stone until he began to feel dizzy.

"Time you learned how to do this," Uncle Perry said, taking his foot off the board and letting the fine-grained stone slow. The swish of water stopped as the stone lost momentum, and Josiah found himself being positioned next to the grindstone. "Start slowly and keep the angle steady," Uncle Perry instructed, handing him a long, dull knife.

Uncle Perry made sharpening look easy, but Josiah struggled to make the wheel turn steadily and to keep the knife blade at the correct angle. At first he was afraid that the knife might be getting duller, not sharper, but he kept at it and, as usual, Uncle Perry hardly said a word. Sometimes he was glad that Uncle Perry mostly let him learn from his own mistakes, but now he realized he didn't know how to tell if the knife was sharp enough. He thought of Alvin's cleaver and wondered if Alvin had sharpened it himself. Sharp enough to cut off a hen's head.

Just then Uncle Perry said, "Time to try the edge and see how it's coming." He took the knife, looked at the blade, and ran it over his thumbnail. "Touch it up on the other side and it'll be sharp enough to butcher a hog."

The sharpened edge of the knife gleamed in the light. I did that, Josiah thought, with a certain pride. I changed it.

Next Uncle Perry gave him an ax head to sharpen. "I'll teach you how to use it, come fall," he said. But the ax made Josiah think of what Aunt Ethel had said about the people of Prescott waiting for "the ax to fall." How could Boston decide to cut off the lives of people in the valley, people like the man who wrote that poem? And why was there so much waiting?

Josiah spent the rest of the morning working at the grindstone. He had a lot of trouble with that first ax head. He kept asking himself, What if Aunt Ethel is wrong and water comes creeping right up to the farm?

Finally he told himself to stop thinking about things he couldn't do anything about and pay attention to what he was doing. Then the sharpening went better. Uncle Perry wasn't there anymore, so Josiah began to test his own edges, and he marveled at how sharp they became.

Right before Aunt Ethel rang the old cowbell for dinnertime, Uncle Perry reappeared and, after watching and checking some edges, announced, "You've got the hang of it now." Coming from Uncle Perry, that was high praise. No matter how pleased he was, Uncle Perry would probably never pat him on the back and say, "Josiah, you've done a great job." But Josiah felt the praise, and he wanted to jump up and down with satisfaction, as if he were a small boy being rewarded with a chocolate. No, it was more than that—it was as if Uncle Perry had said, "We didn't make a mistake in taking you."

14
An Arrowhead

When Josiah came into the kitchen later that afternoon, it was filled with a delicious spicy smell. "Here, have a taste," Aunt Ethel said, scraping a spoonful of sticky red stuff from the sides of an empty kettle. "It's your Grandma Johnson's tomato marmalade recipe."

Josiah took the spoon and licked the marmalade off. Then his tongue went all around his mouth, making sure he hadn't missed any. "This sure beats stewed tomatoes," he commented.

"One of my favorites, too," Aunt Ethel told him. "Now run on over to the Damons' and give this jar to Mrs. Damon. Tell her I said to come over here and sit for a bit when she has a chance."

Josiah took the still-warm pint jar, his fingers closing over the bailing wires that held the glass lid and rubber ring on tight. "Addy told me they might move before school starts. Do you think they will?" he asked.

"I don't rightly know," she answered. "They'd have to sell the farm first and, well, it's not a good time for that." She shook her head and turned away. She's always shaking her head, Josiah thought as he headed out the door.

Seeing the roof of the Damons' barn brought him right back to the day of the storm, but he noticed that Mr. Damon had shored up more of the side of the barn, stabilizing the front part. The broken roof still sat awry to the rear. Their dog, Digger, started to bark at him as he approached the house. Josiah paid no attention, but it made him remember his first night on the farm when he was afraid of Shep. Now he wasn't just a city boy, and he knew that it was the dog's job to bark.

He had hoped to see Addy, but it was Mrs. Damon who came to the kitchen door, the baby clinging to her apron. At the same moment

Addy came bounding around from behind the house, her braids flying. "Adelaide!" her mother called. "Young ladies don't run."

"Yes, Ma. I know," Addy answered, coming to a halt and looking down at her dusty, bare feet. "But I'm not a young lady yet," she added firmly, looking up at her mother.

Josiah caught Addy's eye and couldn't help grinning. He was nearly certain that, among other things, young ladies wouldn't be allowed to go fishing. Suddenly remembering why he was there, he held out the jar of tomato marmalade to Mrs. Damon. "My aunt just made this, and she said for you to come sit a bit with her when you can."

As soon as Mrs. Damon went back into the house, Addy said, "I have something that I want to show you." She reached into her pocket and brought out a small piece of whitish stone. "Do you know what it is?" she asked excitedly.

"Can I hold it?" Josiah asked. In reply, Addy handed him the stone. It was quartz, he could tell, and it was pointed at one end and sort of notched on both sides at the other. "Looks like an arrowhead to me. Where'd you get it?"

"I found it down by the brook, where some animal had been digging. I never would have noticed it if the sun hadn't hit it so it sparkled. It's a real Indian arrowhead!"

"But how did it get here? There aren't any Indians around."

"No, not now. Maybe this arrowhead has been just waiting there for two hundred years. Maybe the Indian shot at something with his bow and arrow, and he missed and the arrowhead has been lost ever since, until I found it. My pa says that the Indians who used to live here were called Nipmucks."

"You mean they lived right here, where we live?" Josiah asked. "I knew Indians were once in Plymouth, when the *Mayflower* landed, and even around Boston long ago. I just never thought about them being here. Why did they leave?"

"I don't know. Maybe they got shot at, with guns, or else they just all died off. I'll ask my pa."

Just then Mrs. Damon's voice came through the screen door. "Addy, Addy! You come on in now and watch the little ones while I get supper ready."

"I guess I have to go. Soon we'll be back in school. Did you hear that we're having a new teacher?" she asked over her shoulder as she disappeared into the kitchen, the screen door slamming behind her.

The stone arrowhead was still in Josiah's hand. He examined it more closely and considered how long it must have taken to chip away at the hard quartz until there was a sharp point. He felt like putting it in his pocket. Instead he called through the screen, "Addy, you forgot your arrowhead!"

Addy came dashing to the door and took it back. "Thanks," she said. "I'm never going to take it to school, because if Alvin ever knew I had a genuine arrowhead he'd steal it fast as greased lightning."

Wishing he could find an arrowhead, Josiah started walking home. Without really thinking about it, he took the longer route through the pastures and over the hill instead of going along the road. He wondered if some Nipmuck boy had once walked where he was walking. Then he found himself running his eyes over the land—the fields, pastures, streams, hills, buildings, everything—as if he were taking possession of it, or rather, as if the land were taking possession of him. I'm going to try drawing a picture of this, he thought, if I can, and maybe, if it's good, I'll show it to Addy.

That night at supper, Josiah asked, "Do you know anything about the Indians who used to live around here?"

"My grandmother said all Indians were savages. I guess she was afraid of them," Aunt Ethel replied. "But why are you asking?"

"Well, Addy Damon found an Indian arrowhead and she says Indians—Nipmucks, she called them—once lived here."

"They hunted and fished here, that's certain," Uncle Perry said. "I think many of them died of sickness—smallpox, measles, that sort of thing—or else they went north or west. Then the last of them picked the wrong side to be on in the French and Indian War."

Josiah nodded as if he knew what the French and Indian War was all about, which he didn't.

"Anyway," Uncle Perry continued, "I guess they could read the handwriting on the wall, even though they couldn't read, once settlers started coming to the valley."

"My brother Albert had a whole collection of arrowheads and other things he found. He was always poking around instead of doing his chores, that one," Aunt Ethel said, a faraway look on her face. "I'll see if I can lay my hands on his box when I have a moment, and I'll show them to you. It's a small wooden box, and I'm sure as certain I didn't throw it out."

"Why, Ethel, of course you didn't throw it out—you knew you were going to need it one day," Uncle Perry said, his expression all serious. Aunt Ethel looked at him and started to smile and then laugh. Suddenly they were all three laughing together.

After things had calmed down and the dishes were washed and put away, Uncle Perry said something else: "If we do have to leave this valley, we won't be the first ones that were forced out." All the warm feeling of laughter left the room, like air coming out of a punctured balloon.

15
Aunt Ethel's Box

A FEW DAYS LATER UNCLE PERRY ANNOUNCED that he was going to drive over to the Slade farm that afternoon to discuss some "business" with Mr. Slade. "You want to come along, Josiah?"

"No, thank you," Josiah replied, thinking of Alvin and the headless hen.

"The Slade boy must be about your age. Isn't he at school with you?"

"Yes, sir, he is. Actually he's older than I am." And bigger, Josiah thought. "But he's behind in his lessons."

Then Aunt Ethel spoke up. "Well, if you're going, you could give me a ride to the Pratts' farm. Old Granny Pratt has been poorly and I'd like to pay a call."

"I'll do that," Uncle Perry agreed. "And I'll pick you up on the way back so as to be home before it's time to milk."

After the sound of old Ned's hooves died away and the buggy was out of sight, Josiah sat down on the stone doorstep. He'd thought he would spend the time making another drawing in his notebook, maybe one of the barn, but now he had another idea. What he wanted to do wasn't exactly wrong, but it wasn't exactly right, either. He decided he'd think about it some more while he was in the garden getting the string beans Aunt Ethel wanted picked.

While he picked, searching among the leaves of the pole bean vines for long, hanging, green beans, he told himself that this was a perfect opportunity. Nobody would ever know what he'd been up to. Soon the basket was full of beans. He put it on the table in the kitchen and found himself back out on the doorstep. Shep came over, bringing a stick that Josiah tossed for him a few times. Then he threw the stick as hard as he could, all the way over the stone wall and into the pasture. Shep bounded after it, disappearing over the wall. Josiah turned, not waiting for the dog to come back, and went into the house. He headed straight to the parlor and pulled open the desk drawer.

He hesitated for a moment before opening the box, telling himself one more time that this box was private, and that he could just go on asking questions. Still, he felt he had to understand what it was that Aunt Ethel didn't want to talk about; to understand about damming the river.

Then his fingers had the cover off the box, and he saw the clipping with the poem lying on top. There were so many pieces of paper, and he imagined that Aunt Ethel knew precisely how they all fit into the box. She'd notice if he disturbed them. He took the poem out, looked at the piece of newspaper on top, and guessed that it was the clipping Mrs. Pratt had just given her. He started to read it, but then he saw his aunt's handwriting and a date. They all had dates, he realized, and they were in order. He should have known that Aunt Ethel, who put the date and contents on each of her jars of jam, jelly, or preserves, would have such a system.

Carefully, he lifted up a batch of clippings. Now the date on top was 1922. He set another batch aside. Then he went for the bottom of the pile and found the date—1895. These must be about something else, he told himself. That's more than thirty years ago!

The 1895 article, from the *Ware River News*, was about a report by the Massachusetts Board of Health, which proposed damming the Nashua River in Boylston to create a reservoir. Josiah didn't know where Boylston was, but the board also proposed extending the system westward to "the valley of the Swift," where a huge, future reservoir could be created. And all this water would go to the city of Boston.

The next article was from 1901, about work on the dam on the Nashua River for the new reservoir and about buildings being "demolished." Suddenly it was real to him—houses torn down, water about to start rising.

He read one from 1908 describing the completion of that reservoir, called the Wachusett Reservoir. Josiah remembered that name from what Mr. Damon had said to him at the Fourth of July picnic. The Wachusett was where Boston's water came from—the water his parents drank when they were alive, the water he drank.

Then in 1909 there were several articles about engineers being present in the Swift River Valley towns and reminding readers of the 1895 plans to dam up the Swift River. Most people, it seemed, didn't believe it would happen. One article noted that it was "safe to say the day is far distant when it will be done. North Dana people don't need to move before snow flies, at any rate." That piece made Josiah feel better, as did some articles suggesting that Boston should consider water sources closer to the city.

For 1919 he found articles describing how the towns in the Swift River Valley—Enfield, Dana, Greenwich, Prescott, and all the villages—were threatened by something called the Joint Board, which was studying the plans for the proposed reservoir. Next came a whole bunch of articles from 1922, including reports on the report of the Joint Board. He read the first one. It said that the creation of the giant reservoir, flooding the towns in the valley, should be approved. He stopped—the article was written years ago, and still nothing seemed to be settled!

Josiah had no stomach for reading any more, and besides, what if Aunt Ethel and Uncle Perry came back early and found him here in the midst of all these papers? Quickly he put the clippings away as he had found them, and shoved the box into the drawer.

Standing for a minute in the parlor, his hands on the back of his ma's rocker, he gazed out the window at the pasture and the hills. He noticed that the cows were already coming into the barnyard, waiting to be milked. He remembered what Aunt Ethel had said about people being tired of waiting. He realized suddenly that they had been waiting ever since that first clipping, back in 1895.

He went into the kitchen and started stringing the beans, snapping the stem ends off and pulling the fine strings of fiber down to the tails, then snapping off the tails. He didn't let himself think while he worked, and he finished the last beans just as the buggy pulled up to the barn.

When Aunt Ethel came into the kitchen and saw the beans all fixed, she said, "My, you've been busy, and I only asked you to pick them. Sometimes I don't know how Uncle Perry and I managed before you came to live with us."

"Well, I knew they needed stringing," Josiah answered, but her kind words made him feel unworthy. What would she have said if she had caught him in the act of going through her private box? He didn't want to think about that or about all those clippings. "I'm going to go out to help with the milking," he said. She gave him a big smile, as if she were thanking him for doing his regular chores, too, which made him feel even worse.

When Josiah got to the barn, Uncle Perry was still busy unharnessing old Ned. The barn was filled with the familiar, even comforting, smells of animals, hay, and manure; Josiah took a deep breath. Then he went to let the cows into the tie-up and started to wash Daisy off, scrubbing her brown-and-white coat and carefully cleaning her udder. Uncle Perry came in, and soon warm milk was hissing into both their pails. The barn cats crept in along the side of the gutter, and Uncle Perry aimed a squirt of milk at the calico cat. She caught it neatly in her open mouth. They finished with the routine of milking and stood together for a moment at the top of the back ramp, watching the cows head out to pasture. Then Uncle Perry said, "Having another pair of hands around is certainly a help. Almost makes me want to fix the place up."

Josiah didn't say anything. Both Aunt Ethel and Uncle Perry appreciating him on one afternoon; it was too much. Somehow it made him miss his parents, and at the same time realize that he'd come to care about Aunt Ethel and Uncle Perry. He looked over the backs of the cows and down toward the brook where they would go to drink, and swallowed hard.

That night at supper Aunt Ethel talked about her visit with the Pratts. "Ellen Pratt says she can't figure out what ails her mother-in-law. Ellen's worried that Granny won't make it through the winter if she doesn't pick up some. I sat with them for a piece, but all old Granny Pratt said was 'I was born on this farm and I intend to die on it.'"

"Did she look that poorly, as if the end were near?" Uncle Perry wanted to know.

"No, I wouldn't say so. Anyway, we told her that there was no rush—that nothing is going to happen for a while yet. So she brightened up a bit, said she hoped not."

So Granny Pratt would rather fade away and die than be moved, Josiah thought to himself. She's afraid of the dam—that's what ails her.

16
The Enemy

It was the end of the first week in September, and Aunt Ethel told Josiah she was sure it would freeze that night. A few days earlier they had covered all the tender plants in the garden with old bed sheets and blankets, keeping a light frost from harming the plants. True, when he went out to the barn to milk, Josiah had noticed a new crispness in the air, but now the sun was up and the sky was a brilliant, cloudless blue. "How do you know it will freeze?" he asked.

"I can feel it," she replied. "The Almanac says not until next Wednesday, but I never put my trust in the Almanac. We need to gather everything in today."

First there were the tomatoes to pick, all the green ones as well as the ripe, red ones. Then the few remaining summer squashes and all the beans that were big enough. Aunt Ethel shook her head over the tiny, baby beans. "It's a shame we don't have another week. Just one more week and they'd be ready to pick."

Next there were glossy peppers and the last of the cucumbers. Josiah lugged basket after basket from the garden to the kitchen. He was hot, and he couldn't imagine that it was really going to freeze. The Almanac is probably right, he thought. At least the carrots, beets, potatoes, turnips, and parsnips were safe under the ground, and the cabbages could stand some frost, along with the winter squashes and pumpkins. He had never known about any of these things when he lived in Boston, and, he realized, he hadn't paid any attention to frost, except that his ma had made him wear a warmer jacket to school. He wondered if his jacket would still fit when school started next week. He more than half wished that school would never start again.

Toward the end of the afternoon, the temperature began to drop, and later, under a bright moon, the wind picked up. When Josiah woke the next morning, white frost covered the roofs and clung to each blade of grass.

A few days later, after witnessing a frenzy of canning and pickling in the kitchen, Josiah spotted Mrs. Damon coming up the drive with Addy and the little girls in tow. Aunt Ethel came out and said how glad she was to have some company, and the two women settled into chairs on the porch, the littlest girls clinging to their mother. Addy and the next oldest girl—Josiah never could remember all their names—came over to where he stood.

"I'm going to school on Monday," the small girl announced. "You and Addy will be going, too. She told me that."

Josiah smiled at her and then looked over at Addy. "I guess we all have to go," he said.

"I can hardly wait to see what the new teacher will be like," Addy replied. "And I'll get to wear my new dress. I wish it were Monday tomorrow."

"Well, I'm glad it's not," Josiah said, thinking of Alvin Slade.

"At least we don't have to move yet, but Pa keeps talking about it," Addy announced.

"I've been wanting to ask you something," Josiah said. "When I first came here, you asked me what I thought about the dam. I didn't understand what you were talking about, and you never would talk about it since." Josiah could feel the red creeping over his face as he remembered how he'd thought she must be imagining it all. "Tell me what you know about the plans to flood the valley, will you?"

"So now you want to really know about it, after all this time," she said, giving him a look. "Well, my pa says they're going to do it. He just doesn't know when. Nobody does—that's why it's so hard to sell a farm now. It's all because of enemy domain, I know that."

"What do you mean, 'enemy domain'? I never heard of it, except that one time when you said it," Josiah answered, wondering if he should have read more clippings. Maybe they explained about this enemy.

"Well, the enemy part is the government in Boston," Addy told him. "They can just take what they want, no matter what we say. Everybody knows that."

Josiah didn't say anything.

"I know something else," Addy went on. "They say that if they flood us out, first they'll move all the dead, before they knock down the houses and everything. They'll dig all the bodies and bones up out of the cemeteries."

Josiah thought back to the day last spring, Memorial Day, when Aunt Ethel had taken him with her to put flowers on Grandpa and Grandma Johnson's graves. He remembered the words carved into his grandfather's stone:

Josiah Johnson
Born 1848 – Died 1911
Rest Here in Peace

And on his grandmother's stone, it said:

Mary Haskell, wife of Josiah Johnson
1857–1909
The Lord Giveth and the Lord Taketh Away

Then there was a small stone that only said *Baby* and *1887*. Nearby, under a tree, was the marker for Daniel Ballard Johnson, his great-grandfather, who had bought the land for the farm and cleared it. From the cemetery, there was a nice view of the hills. Josiah didn't think he wanted his grandparents, or the baby who never got to live, to be dug up.

Then he thought of old Granny Pratt. Even if she died here, right on the farm, even if she was buried in the quiet of the cemetery by the old church, she might still have to leave the valley. They'd move her bones away to somewhere else.

WHILE THEY WERE MILKING LATE THAT AFTERNOON, Josiah decided to talk to Uncle Perry. He didn't want to risk upsetting Aunt Ethel by asking questions at supper. "When Addy Damon was here today, she told me about enemy domain. She says that's why they could dam up the river to make a reservoir."

"Enemy domain? That's a good one," Uncle Perry replied, and then he started to laugh. "Addy said that? Well, she's clever!" And he laughed some more.

Josiah's face, pressed against the cow's flank where Uncle Perry couldn't even see it, began to turn red, and the milk stopped hissing rhythmically into his pail. Had Addy been fooling with him? She'd certainly made a fool of him in front of Uncle Perry.

At last, after Uncle Perry's laughter died away, Josiah said, "Well, that's what she told me," as if that was an excuse.

"She meant **eminent** domain, not enemy, but I think she got it right."

"Eminent?" Josiah repeated. "Eminent domain. But what does that mean?"

"It's part of the law. It means that the government, that's Boston, has the right to take property for the public good. At least that's how they explained it at the hearing I went to back in 1922, in Enfield. There must have been five hundred people there, and we all voted against the plan to dam up the valley, but that doesn't make a particle of difference—they can still do it."

Primrose looked around at Josiah and mooed, as if wondering why he wasn't milking. He couldn't hear any milk squirting into Uncle Perry's pail, either.

"It's like this," Uncle Perry said, his words coming to Josiah between the legs of the cows, "the reservoir they want to build would be for the public good of Boston. It's not for our good. They would take our homes and give us a few dollars in exchange. We don't have the votes here to make the politicians in Boston pay any attention to our good."

"I see," said Josiah. "So Boston is the enemy."

17
Listening on the Stairs

THAT EVENING, SHORTLY AFTER JOSIAH CLIMBED UP THE STEPS to Uncle Albert's old room—his room now—he heard Aunt Ethel and Uncle Perry talking together. "So he won't help, not at all?" she asked.

"Says it's not his problem. Says he offered to buy the whole place right after that storm took the roof half off, but Fred turned him down," Uncle Perry responded.

Josiah crept partway down the stairs to hear better, but stopped before the squeaking step. So this was the "business" that had taken Uncle Perry to see Mr. Slade.

"How much did he offer?" Aunt Ethel inquired. "Probably it wasn't enough to buy a woodshed, let alone a new farm somewhere else, out of the valley."

"Not much, I'd guess. Said he's still willing to buy some of the cows—only the best milkers, of course. I did ask him how much he'd give for a cow like Bessie, and when he told me, I said I wouldn't take that for a goat. No wonder Fred wouldn't sell."

"Well, I don't see how the Damons are going to manage through the winter. But I should have known better than to think Ira Slade would help," Aunt Ethel said. "Albert and I went to school with him, you know. He was a bully then, but we all thought it was because his pa took the strap to him something terrible. Just like chickens with their pecking order, he had to take it out on someone else. I wonder if he lays into that boy of his," she mused.

Josiah remembered the day he took Buttercup to the Slades' farm. Mr. Slade's forearms were as thick as his own thighs. He'd never noticed a mark on Alvin, but Aunt Ethel's remark made him consider.

"In any case," Uncle Perry said, "Fred's too proud to ask for any assistance. Keeps saying he won't take charity. But maybe John Pratt and I can persuade him to let some of us give him a hand with the barn, finish making most of it safe enough to use, at least until spring. He can't leave the cows out all winter and milk them in the woodshed."

"I know Ida doesn't want to move now, at least not to go live with Fred's brother and his family in New Hampshire," Aunt Ethel said. "But unless they can sell the farm, they won't have money enough to do anything else. And I think Ida's in the family way again, although she hasn't said so."

"If she is, that would be seven girls!" Uncle Perry's response came up the steps.

"What makes you so sure it would be another girl? Just because Daisy's had seven bull calves in a row, while you were hoping each time for a heifer! Well, it would be another mouth to feed and all . . ." Aunt Ethel's words trailed off.

"Time we got some sleep. Nothing we can do about this tonight."

JOSIAH WAITED FOR A FEW MOMENTS ON THE DARK STAIRS and then crept quietly back up to his room and into bed. Moonbeams streamed in through the small-paned windows and made a pattern on the old quilt. He lay awake, thinking about the Damons. He hoped they wouldn't leave the valley, especially not Addy. What if everybody really does have to leave? he thought. What if I have to move again? And where would I go this time? Would Aunt Ethel and Uncle Perry take me with them? They don't have any kin anywhere to take them in, except maybe for Uncle Albert, and they don't even know whether he's alive or dead.

18
Back to School

Hurrying through his morning barn chores, Josiah couldn't help thinking about school. Today was the first day, and he didn't want to go. It was as simple as that.

Coming into the house, he snuck past Aunt Ethel, who was busy at the stove, and climbed the stairs two at a time. Back in his room, he tugged on a pair of pants that he hadn't worn all summer, pulled on some socks, and jammed his feet into his only pair of shoes. His feet were well calloused from going barefoot all summer, and they seemed to have changed in shape and size. He got the buttons on a school shirt done up, but it felt tight all over, like a skin that he needed to shed. At least it was warm enough so that he wouldn't need his jacket.

What good is school anyway? Josiah asked himself. I didn't learn a thing there last year. Why should I go? He stamped his way down the stairs, making his toes hurt. They're packed like sardines wedged into a can, he thought as he came scowling into the kitchen.

"You've grown!" Aunt Ethel announced, her eyes traveling the length of him. "Pants too short," she muttered to herself. "Should have seen to that before, at least let the hems down. I'm sure my sister would have." She put his plate of eggs and toast on the table.

Josiah stared at the two unblinking yolk eyes of the eggs.

"You have to eat something before you go, though I've already fixed a lunch pail for you," Aunt Ethel said. "They'll get cold," she added, nodding toward the eggs.

"I just don't feel hungry," Josiah remarked. Plunking himself into the chair, he examined the toast. Aunt Ethel must have held the bread carefully over the coals with her toasting fork, he thought, because it wasn't burned at all. When he tried to make toast, it always came out pale or charred or both. And it was spread with butter and strawberry jam—usually jam was only for Sundays. He picked up the toast.

"As I remember, the first day of school was always worst before it started. It won't be so bad once you get there."

"Maybe," Josiah answered between bites of egg and toast. "But maybe not." He thought of Alvin; perhaps it would be worse. Of course, there was Addy. And then there would be the new teacher.

It had rained during the night, so the road was muddy, with ruts and potholes filled with water. Josiah considered taking off his pinching shoes but decided he didn't want Alvin, or even Addy, to know his shoes pinched. They'd see his too-short pants anyway, not that Addy would care. Then he saw Addy and her sister waiting for him at the bottom of their turn-in.

Addy had on a new dress, maybe the one she had picked blueberries for, and she held her little sister by the hand. "Morning," Josiah and Addy said at once, a bit stiffly, almost as if they didn't know each other.

"Leena, say good morning," Addy prompted her sister.

"G'morning," Leena said, so softly that Josiah could barely hear. For a moment nobody seemed able to find anything to say next. Then words came tumbling out of Addy: "I heard that the new teacher doesn't know anything about anything—and he's a man!"

"Can't believe everything you hear," Josiah answered.

"Well, I'm going to ask him just what he does know, so then the whole school will find out," she retorted.

"You can't do that; he's the teacher. You better not start by asking questions in school," Josiah told her, laughing and feeling more like himself. But Addy turned red and didn't say anything more. "Come on, Leena," she said, tugging her sister ahead of Josiah.

He didn't say anything either until the Pratt boys joined them. And as they came around the next bend, Josiah knew the moment when Alvin would come down the lane from the Slade farm was almost upon him. But Alvin wasn't there. Maybe he's not coming, Josiah thought. Maybe he decided to quit school.

Soon they could hear the noise of the schoolyard, and then they turned in at the gate. Still no sign of Alvin. Josiah felt himself start to smile as he skirted an enormous mud puddle that sat like a lake in the roadway. Suddenly someone pushed him hard from behind, right into Addy and then, splash, into the great puddle. He looked up and there was Alvin. "Thought you might need a bath, Boston Boy, since you don't have a bathtub anymore," he sneered. "How do you like our nice, clean water?"

Josiah's knee felt a stab of pain, and out of the corner of his eye he saw his lunch floating in the mud puddle. In front of him, Addy pulled herself up, her dress dripping mud. Addy looked madder than a wet hen, and her sister was crying. Josiah got to his feet and ran at Alvin, both fists raised. Alvin backed away, his fists up, and some of the other boys started to yell, "Fight! Fight!"

At that instant a stocky young man came running toward them, holding the school bell. It's the new teacher, Josiah realized, and lowered his fists. But the man was behind Alvin, who didn't see him, and Alvin let fly with a punch that landed with a hard thump on Josiah's chest. Josiah went down in a heap. Addy rushed forward, furiously kicking at Alvin's shins. The teacher's hands closed firmly on Alvin's shoulders, the bell dropping to the ground with a clank.

"Enough," the teacher ordered. "You," he said, jerking his chin at Josiah as Alvin twisted under his hands, "go wash at the pump. You, too," he added, shaking his head and looking at Addy, "and clean up the little one as best you can." He tightened his grip on Alvin's shoulders and announced, "I will not have fighting at my school."

He marched Alvin off toward the schoolhouse, pupils scattering out of their way. Josiah, getting to his feet, noticed that Alvin was nearly as tall as the teacher.

SOON THE BELL RANG AGAIN and the pupils poured into the schoolhouse. When they had all found seats, the teacher proclaimed, "There will be no pushing, shoving, or fighting at this school! Is that clear?" An intense quiet filled the schoolroom.

"I am Mr. Richardson, your new teacher. I only arrived from Vermont yesterday, so I haven't had time to go over the books and other supplies at this school, but I'm sure we will find what we need. Now I will call the roll." Mr. Richardson took up a sheet of paper with a list on it and started calling out the students' names.

Josiah fidgeted at his desk, sensing Alvin sitting right behind him and seeing Addy, her braids hanging down her mud-stained dress, at a desk on his right. The older Pratt boy, Tom, was on his left. Leena, sitting in the front row with the other little ones, still gave a small sob from time to time.

"David Dobbins." The name hung in the air as the teacher looked around the room, waiting for a response. "Lucy Dobbins." Nothing. "Caleb Dobbins?" Again silence. Addy raised her hand, and the teacher nodded to her.

"Sir, the Dobbinses all left the valley."

They could hear his pen crossing those names off the list. A bit later he came to William and Annie Morris. Again silence and again Addy's hand went up. "They've left already. Moved away, on account of how things are," Addy told the teacher.

"Well, how are things?" the teacher asked.

For once Addy seemed tongue-tied.

Alvin blurted out, "I guess you don't know any more about this valley than Boston Boy does. They're going to dam up the Swift River and make a flood. My pa says they won't flood everything though, not the high parts, not our farm."

"Alvin Slade, you will not speak in school unless I call on you," the teacher ordered. "Now, I will find out what all of you learned last year in school."

The rest of the morning was spent with the teacher quizzing each student in reading and arithmetic. Then they were dismissed for lunch. Tom Pratt handed Josiah half of his bread and cheese. "Here," he said. "I saw your lunch floating in that mud puddle."

Josiah thanked him and took the sandwich. They sat quietly, chewing, and then Tom said, "Last year, before you came, Alvin had a big fight with David Dobbins. They both got bloody noses and David's arm was nearly broken. He lost." Josiah looked around for Alvin and saw him standing by himself near the schoolhouse. Addy sat with Leena and the other girls.

Soon the bell rang and Mr. Richardson handed out books. "Some of you will have to share," he said, "and I will need to order new books for others. I was planning to teach Latin to you older ones, but there don't seem to be any Latin books at all."

A hand went up. "Sir, they only teach Latin in high school here."

Behind him, Alvin muttered, "Latin's no use to anybody." But Josiah wondered what it would be like to know Latin, what he might be missing.

Finally school was dismissed for the day. As he left the schoolyard, Josiah saw Alvin walking ahead. Addy was behind him, dragging Leena along to catch up. Alvin turned around to face Josiah. "Don't think that teacher can protect you, Boston Boy. He can't stop me from fighting out of school!"

WHEN JOSIAH GOT BACK TO THE FARMHOUSE, he saw Aunt Ethel standing on the little porch outside the kitchen door as if she were waiting for him, just the way his ma used to wait for him on the stoop of their apartment building, and suddenly he missed his ma terribly, as if he were a little boy again.

No chance now to slip by Aunt Ethel without any questions. She looked him up and down, no doubt taking in the torn knee of his muddied pants as well as the mud stains on his shirt. "Those pants need to be let down at the hem, and I'll patch that tear while I'm at it," she said. "Go on up and take them off—I'll have to wash them first—and bring me down your other pair so I can let them down, too."

Josiah could hardly believe it. Not a single question about school or about how his pants got ripped. He went up the stairs two at a time, shucked off the pants, flung them at the floor right below the window, and pulled on a comfortable old pair, short and already well patched. Picking up the torn pants, he noticed that he had knocked a piece of the baseboard loose. Down on his hands and knees, he started to push the board back into place, but it fell out, exposing an open space in the wall.

Peering into the opening, he saw a marble and a metal thing. In an instant the marble was in his hand, and then the metal object. With his head touching the floor, he saw more marbles, one of them a big agate. An old hiding place of Uncle Albert's!

He scooped out the marbles, and they rolled about on the floor until he chased them all down and put them into a drawer. Then he turned his attention to the other object and saw at once that it was a harmonica. He wiped the dust of years off it and onto his shirt. He blew into it, admiring the sound, and on the way down the stairs he blew some more, trying it out.

At the bottom of the stairs, Josiah almost ran into Aunt Ethel, her hand clutched to her chest. "Lands above! When I heard that harmonica, I thought for a moment Albert was back with us. I didn't know that you had a harmonica."

"I never did, but a friend at school used to let me borrow his."

By the time that Josiah finished explaining about finding the hiding place, Aunt Ethel had calmed down. "I always believed that Albert took his harmonica with him when he left. I know he took your Grandpa Johnson's fiddle. Everybody loved to hear him play that fiddle, and all the girls were sweet on him." She stopped for a moment, as if she were listening to her brother playing a tune. Then she turned to Josiah. "After your ma died, I wrote to Albert at the last address we had for him, but there's been no answer. I just wanted you to know that." Then she looked away, out the window.

Not sure what to say, Josiah offered up his torn pants, telling her, "I fell into a mud puddle."

"I see," answered Aunt Ethel, giving him a knowing look.

"Did Uncle Albert ever get into fights at school?"

"Heavens, yes. He'd come home with black eyes and torn clothes. Actually, I don't think he fought in school; the teacher was strict. It was after school. Your Grandma Johnson, my ma, she used to shake her head and say she didn't know what would become of him." Aunt Ethel hesitated, and then added, "And we probably never will know."

For the rest of that week of school, Josiah remained on his guard, always watching out for Alvin. The new teacher kept them all busy. He was quite a change from Miss Cooper and didn't seem to mind answering questions, even Addy's. He let Josiah skip two readers and move ahead in the next one at his own pace.

It would have been fun to bring the harmonica to school, to show it to Addy and the Pratt boys and play it during the lunch recess, even though he couldn't play very well. But Josiah remembered what Addy had said about her arrowhead and Alvin, and he didn't want to risk losing the mouth organ. It would be safer at home.

Many of the boys had marbles, so Josiah put a few small ones in his pocket to take to school. One he lost to Tom Pratt, fair and square, but the other two ended up in Alvin's pocket. Alvin had cheated; everybody saw him do it. "Hey, that's not fair!" Josiah exclaimed. All the boys looked at Alvin, but Alvin just smirked and didn't give the marbles back. Josiah shoved his fists into his pockets and decided not to make an issue of it—and not to bring any more marbles to school. No point in asking for trouble, his ma would have said. But all the rest of the day he was mad at himself.

19
Apples and Things

That weekend, they were going to pick apples and make the first cider. Uncle Perry got the cider press ready, and Aunt Ethel talked about canning applesauce and making apple butter. "Your grandfather planted most of the orchard," Aunt Ethel told Josiah, rattling off a long list of apple varieties—Baldwin, Pippin, Sheepnose, Roxbury Russet, Greening, and Seek-No-Further. "Those trees will go on bearing for many years, at least they will if . . ." She didn't finish the sentence, but by now Josiah understood what the "if" meant.

Saturday morning found them all in the orchard with the apple ladder, long pole pickers, and plenty of baskets and wooden boxes. Uncle Perry went up the ladder, filled a big bag that hung from his shoulders and was tied around his waist, climbed down, emptied the bag gently into a box or basket, and went up to pick another bagful.

Meanwhile, Aunt Ethel instructed Josiah in using an apple picker. The idea was to thrust the long pole, with its small wire basket at the top, up into the tree, aiming for an apple. He was to do this carefully so as not to knock off any apples, because if they fell they might be bruised. "Enough apples fall off as it is, without our helping them," she said. Once he maneuvered the apple into the wire basket, he was supposed to give another little thrust to separate the apple's stem from its branch. Sometimes two or even three apples would fit into the wire basket before the picker was lowered to take out the apples. But Josiah kept having trouble directing the pole, and soon Aunt Ethel tied a bag onto him and sent him scrambling up a tree to pick what he could reach. He grabbed for an apple, stretching his fingers to reach it, and found himself hanging by one arm, feet kicking in the air. *This isn't as easy as it looks either*, he thought as he managed to pull himself up to safety.

They picked all morning, Josiah munching on apples from time to time, their sweet juice running down his chin. In the afternoon they sorted the apples: some for cooking, the best for storage, and the rest for cider.

"Now we have to make the cheese," Aunt Ethel said.

"Cheese? We aren't making cheese today, are we?"

Aunt Ethel gave a little laugh. "Yes and no. We get the apples all grated up before we layer them into the cider press. The grated apples are called cheese. We'll let the cheese sit overnight and make the cider tomorrow."

In the morning Uncle Perry loaded the strong, slatted press with the apple cheese and began to turn the wheel, squeezing down on the apples inside and making the juice run out between the wooden slats and into the bottom. Soon there was cider ready to be poured into jugs.

One old apple tree stood by itself, leaning over the pasture fence near where the cows waited before they came up the ramp and into the barn. Josiah went to see if it had any apples worth picking. Most of them were still green. As he watched the cows search for fallen apples under the tree, one cow caught his attention. Why was Daisy standing that odd way, with her sides heaving and her head down? There was something wrong with that cow! He ran to get Uncle Perry, who hurried into the pasture.

"You're right, she's in trouble," Uncle Perry said as he led the reluctant, heaving cow through the gate and up into the barnyard, scattering hens as they went. He ran his hands slowly up and down the cow's neck and pointed to a bulge halfway down.

Wiping her hands on her apron, Aunt Ethel came out of the house and joined them around the cow. "Perry, what's wrong with her?"

"She's got something stuck here—I don't know what. I'm going to see if holding her head up will make it go down." Daisy struggled as Uncle Perry raised her head higher and higher. The lump didn't budge.

"Maybe if she'll drink some water, it'll wash down," Aunt Ethel suggested.

"I'll get a pail of water," Josiah volunteered. But Daisy refused to drink and heaved miserably with each breath.

"What could she have swallowed?" Aunt Ethel asked for the third time.

"A cow wouldn't eat a stone, would she?" Josiah asked, staring at Daisy's neck.

"Never heard of such a thing," Aunt Ethel snapped. She hardly ever snapped at him, so Josiah knew that she was seriously worried.

"But she'd eat an apple, wouldn't she. And if she forgot to chew and ate it whole, then it might get stuck . . . ," Josiah suggested.

Uncle Perry's face lit up. "You could have something there, you might indeed." He felt Daisy's neck again. At that moment Daisy collapsed, her legs buckling under her, leaving her lying on her side. Uncle Perry disappeared into the barn, returning at once with two small boards and a mallet.

"I'm going to try to break the apple in two. Of course there's a risk—maybe it's not an apple, or I might crush her windpipe. I might kill her, but she'll die anyway if we don't do something soon." Quickly Uncle Perry slid one piece of wood under the cow's neck where the lump was and got Josiah to hold the second piece on the top. Bang! He hit the board Josiah was holding, and the cow jerked her head up.

After a few strong heaves, Daisy swallowed a couple of times, took great sucking breaths, and finally got to her feet. Aunt Ethel hugged Josiah.

THAT NIGHT AT SUPPER UNCLE PERRY TOLD A STORY about when he was a boy growing up on a farm in Erving. "That year we were raising a whole bunch of pigs. It was late in the fall and we had finished in the orchard, picked our apples and made cider, and some of it was good, hard cider. Anyhow, one morning my pa turned all those pigs out into the orchard to eat whatever they found. That afternoon I was taking a shortcut through the orchard on my way to a neighbor's farm when I saw the pigs acting crazy—some of them were running around on wobbly legs, some squealing, some lying down.

"I ran back to tell my pa and he came running. We went into the orchard and saw all those pigs weaving about. 'The devil's got into the swine!' he said. I watched the pigs rooting around the apple trees and eating all the old windfall apples. Suddenly I said, 'Pa, it's not the devil, it's the apples. They're like hard cider.' My pa didn't like to be corrected, but he sniffed at the apples, then looked at those crazy pigs and laughed.

'Those apples fermented, turned to alcohol, and the pigs are drunk!' he said. Of course, then we had to round up the pigs and get them out of the orchard to sober up. That was no easy job, and I never did get to the neighbor's that day."

"I didn't know that cider would do that to you," Josiah exclaimed, glancing at the glass he had just drained.

"Don't worry," Uncle Perry assured him. "This cider won't, at least not until it ages and gets 'hard.' Then it will pack a punch."

A punch. That made Josiah think of Alvin—he packed a punch, a hard punch. But thinking of Alvin reminded him of something else, of a question he wanted answered. Now wasn't the right time, not with Aunt Ethel sitting there smiling at him, telling him that he'd have to "age" before he drank hard cider.

The next morning, standing in the barn, Josiah asked Uncle Perry about what Alvin had said at school. "Is it true that if they flood the valley, the water won't come this high?"

Uncle Perry gave him a long look and chewed on a hay stem. "It might, and yet again it might not," he replied.

What kind of an answer is that? Josiah thought. It's no help at all. He took a deep breath and asked, "But if we wouldn't be flooded, then we wouldn't have to move, would we? Alvin Slade says the water won't rise as high as their farm, and we're higher, I think."

The color of Uncle Perry's eyes seemed to change, as if some light went out of them, sort of like the sky when the clouds come. He didn't say anything for a moment, and Josiah began to think that he wouldn't. Then Uncle Perry began to speak, "If they decide to do it, then the hilltops will become islands, rising out of the water. And they won't want any people here or houses or towns or cows, nothing. They won't want anyone living around the edges either, because then the water wouldn't be pure enough to send to Boston." He spit out the hay stem and stomped out of the barn. Josiah wished he hadn't asked.

20
A Whistling Girl

THE NEXT WEEK, SCHOOL WENT SMOOTHLY until after dismissal on Thursday. Little Leena tugged on Addy's skirt as they left the schoolyard. "Can you whistle 'Mary Had a Little Lamb' for me? Please, please." Addy started whistling softly.

"Louder, Addy, the way you do behind the barn at home," Leena coaxed.

Addy whistled loudly, her hand in Leena's, their arms swinging together in time with their steps and the song. Josiah, walking behind them, wondered what it might have been like to have a little brother, even a sister.

Alvin, who was walking ahead, halted suddenly, turning and blocking the way. Addy stopped whistling. "A whistling girl and a crowing hen, each will come to some bad end," Alvin jeered at her, and then repeated the rhyme.

"Will not!" Addy replied. "Sticks and stones can break my bones, but words will never hurt me!" she added for good measure. Alvin picked up a stick.

Before he could think about getting into trouble, Josiah scooped up a stone and held it ready to throw. Alvin hurled the stick, just missing Leena. She started to cry. Josiah threw his stone, but Alvin dodged at the last instant.

Addy grabbed up the stick and rushed at Alvin, yelling, "Bully! You're a big bully, Alvin Slade!"

To Josiah's surprise, Alvin just stood there as Addy whacked at him. Then he grabbed the stick and broke it in two, tossing the pieces at Addy's feet. "You're not worth bothering with," he told her. "Besides, my pa told me never to fight with girls," he added as he set off at a fast walk. Josiah started breathing again, but he picked up another stone just in case Alvin changed his mind. Addy soothed Leena and then started to whistle "Yankee Doodle" as loudly as she could.

They were nearing the Damons' farm before Addy, rather out of breath, stopped whistling. "Can you whistle? I never heard you do it," she questioned Josiah.

"Well, I can whistle, though I'm not very good at tunes," Josiah responded. "But I have a harmonica and I've been trying a few songs on it." Then he told her how he had found the harmonica and what Aunt Ethel had said about Uncle Albert and the fiddle.

"I bet your Uncle Albert is playing that fiddle for the motion pictures somewhere. Maybe you can hear him on a Victrola. I wish we had a Victrola—I've never even heard one yet. My sister Betty has, and she says it's wonderful, as if a whole band, with all the instruments, is right inside that wooden box. There's a kind with a crank—you crank it and the music comes out—but Ma says it costs a fortune. Did you have a Victrola when you lived in Boston?"

Josiah was in the middle of trying to imagine Uncle Albert standing in front of an audience, with all the people clapping—Uncle Albert with a twirled mustache, holding Grandpa Johnson's fiddle under his chin. So it took him a moment to answer Addy. "We didn't have a Victrola, but our neighbor did, and we used to listen to songs and opera, but not to my Uncle Albert."

"How do you know?" Addy persisted. "Suppose he was playing the fiddle while somebody sang. Maybe he's rich and famous by now."

"Addy," Josiah said, "if he were famous, we would have heard of him, right?"

"I was just supposing, that's all," Addy answered, sticking her lower lip out as if she were Leena's age. They walked in silence, just the wind in the trees, birds calling, a distant cow lowing, and the bark of a dog somewhere. When they reached the turn-in, Josiah said, "You can try my harmonica sometime if you like, but I'm not bringing it to school."

"I understand about that. I suppose Alvin would take it somehow," Addy replied. "But if you're coming on Saturday to help with the barn, you could bring it then."

"Uncle Perry told me about fixing up your barn. He said that I might be of some use, but mostly I'll have to stay out from under foot. I'll bring the harmonica."

"Where do you think your Uncle Albert is now?"

"Out west somewhere. My Aunt Ethel doesn't know exactly where," Josiah answered.

"Do you suppose he'll ever come back here to the valley? Suppose he comes back and finds it all flooded and all the people gone?"

"Addy, will you just stop supposing!" Josiah exclaimed. But as he walked the rest of the way home, he couldn't help wondering how it would be if Uncle Albert did come back and found a reservoir where home used to be. And where would he and Aunt Ethel and Uncle Perry be by then? Did the city of Boston really need so much more water?

21
Fixing Up

The damons' drive was already filling up with horses and wagons, some loaded with lumber, when Josiah and Uncle Perry arrived. Men whom Josiah didn't know were milling about, but then he spotted Mr. Pratt and the Pratt boys. At the sound of a motorcar coming, he and Tom and Nat sprinted toward the road. A banged-up Ford truck chugged to a stop, and Dick Hutchins and his father got out. Dick was the oldest boy at school—old enough to be in high school. He grinned at them, and Josiah noticed that there were razor nicks all over his chin. The boys trooped over to the barn.

Josiah's eyes ran this way and that. At least there was no sign of Alvin or Mr. Slade, but where was Addy? Her mother must be keeping her in the house, getting her to watch her little sisters or help with the cooking, he thought. It seemed that girls always had to do those things, even if, like Addy, they would rather go fishing. Feeling for the harmonica in his pocket, Josiah guessed that Addy would manage to get out of the house as soon as she could.

Mr. Pratt and Uncle Perry got the men organized, and soon big beams were being lifted into position to brace the side of the barn. There was a lot of talk about what was safe and what they didn't want to risk, particularly when it came to patching the badly damaged section of the roof.

They put up a tall ladder, and while the men were all busy debating, Dick climbed the rungs and got right up on the roof. Josiah saw him perched up there and was worried that Dick didn't know what he was doing. He glanced around for Mr. Hutchins but didn't see him.

"Dick," Josiah called. "Be careful! You could slip!" Dick waved, smiling his big, goofy smile. Suddenly his pa was there, yelling at Dick, "You come right down! Careful how you put your feet!" Startled, Dick lost his balance and started to slide. At the same instant, Josiah and Mr. Hutchins ran to brace the ladder. Josiah, his heart skipping a beat, thought that Dick would fall right off the roof, but the ladder, now held by more hands, caught him at the edge.

Slowly Dick descended while they held the ladder so that it wouldn't tumble. At the bottom he stepped off with a sheepish look. A tide of red crept over his face, just the way it did at school when he didn't know the answer or when Alvin called him stupid.

"Lucky thing you spotted him," Mr. Hutchins said to Josiah. "I'd better take him home before there's a real accident." The whole thing made Josiah think of near misses, of how sometimes things only almost happen.

As the morning wore on, the air rang with the sounds of hammering and of calls for more nails or boards or shingles. The men finally decided to throw an enormous canvas tarp over the worst end of the roof, tie it down well, and leave it at that.

By the time the sun was overhead, Josiah and the Pratt boys were tuckered out from fetching and carrying and staying out of the way. Mrs. Damon rang a cowbell for the dinner break, and everyone gathered by the long table made of planks set on saw horses. Aunt Ethel, who had come to help Mrs. Damon and Betty ready dinner, waved to Josiah as she brought out pitchers of cider. He saw Addy bringing platters of food, but there was no chance to speak to her. Soon he and Tom and Nat were busy eating. Listening as he ate, Josiah heard the men talking about how they would have fixed the barn in the old days. "Just because its roof blew off doesn't mean it might not stand for another hundred years if we fixed it right," said one neighbor. "I still say we ought to fix all of it proper. We could even put a tin roof on it."

"No point," Mr. Damon said, not for the first time that day. "They're having more hearings in Boston, but we know which way the wind is blowing, and we'll all be leaving this valley."

"I heard that there's this government fellow, a Mr. Gow, who says Boston would have plenty of water if they just fixed the leaky pipes and used the reservoirs they have," another man commented.

"That would cost much less, but I heard that they would have to filter the water to make it clean enough to drink, and people in Boston don't want to drink filtered water. They want our water," someone else added.

"Whatever you hear, it's just rumor," Mr. Pratt said. "The report of that Investigating Committee isn't out yet."

With his hand halfway to his mouth, Josiah stopped eating. Why did he have to be from Boston? And, if what the man said was true, why couldn't Boston fix its pipes and filter its water?

Suddenly Addy was at his elbow. "Did you bring it?" she asked.

"Bring what?"

"You said you'd show me your harmonica, the one that was your Uncle Albert's. Did you forget it? And you never show me any of your drawings, either."

"Oh. I was thinking about something else, that's all. I have the harmonica in my pocket," he answered, still thinking about Boston. Maybe this dam thing would only be a near miss. "I'll show it to you later," he said. Addy tossed her braids and left.

By mid-afternoon the men were satisfied with their work and began to leave. It was time to go home to milk. As Uncle Perry and Aunt Ethel were saying their good-byes to the Damons, Addy ran up to Josiah. "I'm so tired of being cooped up in the kitchen and everything," she said. "Can I see the harmonica now?" Josiah pulled the instrument out of his pocket and handed it to her. She admired it for a moment and then started to put it to her lips.

"You better not try playing it—you might sound like a crowing hen," Josiah warned. He smiled, but Addy didn't. Without a moment's further hesitation, she put the harmonica to her mouth and blew it hard. A loud blast of music came out, and then she made the harmonica run up and down its scales from one end to the other.

"Mercy," Mrs. Damon exclaimed. "Adelaide, whatever are you thinking?"

Josiah saw Aunt Ethel smothering a chuckle and guessed that harmonicas must indeed be about as bad as whistling for girls. Addy returned the harmonica with a big smile.

On their way home Aunt Ethel asked if she could see the harmonica. Josiah handed it to her and at first she just held it, examining it as if it were a precious jewel. "Albert never let me play with it. He said that harmonicas were only for boys, but I think I'll try playing it now." And she did, rather softly, before giving it back.

Josiah saw Uncle Perry give Aunt Ethel a funny look, as if he didn't know what to think of his wife. "Glad Fred finally agreed to let us give him a hand," he said, changing the subject away from harmonicas and Albert.

"Ida was right pleased," Aunt Ethel replied. "She says that now she can face the winter. Fred seems determined to leave the valley, though, after the baby comes. They've been good neighbors, and I'll miss them if they go."

Maybe the Damons won't go, Josiah thought. Maybe Boston will decide it's too expensive to build a reservoir here and have to get the water all the way to there.

22
Ready for Winter

THE DAYS GOT SHORTER, THE NIGHTS COOLER, and the trees changed color. In Boston, red, orange, and yellow leaves had cluttered the sidewalks, but here in the valley a patchwork of color blanketed whole hills and edged the fields. The ancient sugar maples lining the road to school deepened in color from one day to the next—a sight, as Aunt Ethel said, beautiful enough to take your breath away.

In school, Addy questioned Mr. Richardson about this transformation. He answered as best he could, something about chlorophyll, and added, "I'm not much of a botanist, but I will try to find out more."

On the farm there was a great, unwritten list of things to be done—a harvest list.

Dig potatoes, carrots, and parsnips. Uncle Perry swore that parsnips tasted best after they had been frozen a bit, so they piled leaves and hay over some rows and left those to dig later.

Bring cabbages to the root cellar.

Pick and shell dried beans. The beans slithered and popped out of the curling pods, and there was a wonderful slippery feel to them, like touching the belly of a snake.

Store pumpkins. The big ones for cows went into the barn, and pie pumpkins were put away in the shed or up in the attic.

Store winter squashes—bulbous, tan ones and large, rumpled, blue ones.

Corncobs to the corncrib.

Every day they did some of it.

There were also the mangels to be harvested from a strip beside the cornfield. All summer Josiah had watched the mangels grow. They started out looking like regular beets, or maybe turnips or even radishes, but they kept on growing bigger and bigger until they were, in fact, gigantic. They pushed themselves up out of the ground, up to two feet tall and nearly as round, with leaves bunching out at the top. Now they needed to come loose from the earth, have their tops cut, and be transported to the root cellar by the barn. The cows would eat them during the winter.

IT WAS SUNDAY, and on Sundays Aunt Ethel often went to church, leaving Uncle Perry and Josiah at home. Unless there was a wedding or a funeral, it was Uncle Perry's view that he could do all the worshiping he needed in the fields and forests of creation. In Boston, Josiah's parents had sometimes taken him to church, and at first Aunt Ethel asked him if he would like to go with her. The very mention reminded him of being at his parents' funeral, so he said no, and soon she stopped asking.

After Aunt Ethel left, sitting straight in the buggy and clucking to old Ned, Uncle Perry and Josiah got on with the harvesting—with getting everything ready for cold and snow.

Today they were going to harvest honey. Mr. Pratt loaned out his honey separator each fall, and it was Uncle Perry's turn to use it. The separator, a barrel-like contrivance, already sat in the kitchen. Josiah had never paid much attention to the beehives, although at first he was afraid the bees might sting him as they buzzed about, going from flower to flower. "You mind your business and they'll mind their business," Aunt Ethel had assured him. At breakfast that morning, Uncle Perry had told Josiah about the inside of a beehive and about the dances that bees do when they return to the hive with pollen.

"Now," Uncle Perry said, "I have to get my bee costume on, and get my hive tool and the smoker." He left Josiah by the barn and headed for the house. Josiah was mystified; he had never seen Uncle Perry smoke, not even a pipe or a cigar.

When Uncle Perry came out, he wore a brimmed hat with a veil hanging all around and tucked into his shirt collar. His pants were tucked into his socks, and gloves covered his hands. In one gloved hand, he held a sort of spouted pot that belched smoke. That must be the smoker, Josiah thought.

They approached the beehives. "You stand back, Josiah. The smoke will calm the bees some, but you don't want to get stung." Uncle Perry puffed smoke at the hives and then used his hive tool, a flat piece of metal with a curved end, to pry the cover off one of the hives. Angry bees buzzed out, and Uncle Perry smoked them again. Bees crawled all over his hat, clung to the veil, and settled on his arms. Watching from a safe distance, Josiah realized that without this "bee costume," Uncle Perry might be covered with stings. When the bees quieted, Uncle Perry lifted out the first super, a boxlike frame that held the honeycomb. Then he took his gloved hand and very gently brushed all the bees off the honeycomb in the super. With a few bees trailing behind, he carried the frame into the kitchen.

"We have to leave some honey in the hives for the bees to eat over the winter," Uncle Perry remarked. "If we don't leave enough, they'll starve. They won't be able to keep the queen warm, and none of them will make it through the winter."

"I never knew, when I lived in Boston, that there was so much to learn and so much to be done on a farm," Josiah said seriously.

"Well, now you know," Uncle Perry replied, with a bit of a chuckle. "I hope you're not too much like Albert. From what Ethel says, he couldn't wait to leave this place."

"I don't ever want to leave," Josiah said. He hadn't meant to say it, but he suddenly knew it was true.

Uncle Perry only nodded, taking a sharp knife and, with a few strokes, slicing the caps off all the little beeswax hexagons in one of the frames. Next he fitted the frame into the separator and set it to spinning inside the wooden barrel. When all the frames but one had been spun, he announced that they were done and pulled the plug out of the hole at the bottom of the barrel, allowing the amber-colored honey to flow out and into jars.

"What about the other frame?" Josiah asked.

"Saving that for comb honey, my favorite. Didn't you ever have honeycomb in Boston?" Josiah shook his head. "Here, have a taste," Uncle Perry offered, cutting a bite of comb honey out of the frame and holding it out on the point of his knife.

Josiah took the honey off the end of the knife and swirled it around in his mouth—delicious! Then he licked his fingers.

"Let's get these supers out of your aunt's kitchen and back into the hives."

They did not finish before Aunt Ethel returned, but she hardly seemed to notice, nor did she say anything about the glowing jars of honey on the table. It wasn't until suppertime that she told them what was bothering her. "There was a lot of talk today after church, and there may be a meeting at the Grange Hall later this week." Josiah hoped that Uncle Perry would ask about the talk and the meeting, but he was eating comb honey spread on bread. Finally Josiah plunged in. "Were they talking about whether they're going to dam up the river?"

It was a moment before Aunt Ethel answered. "Yes, they were."

Uncle Perry finished his honey and pushed back his chair. So that's that, Josiah thought. I'm not going to find out anything more. He frowned at his empty plate, ready to get up, when Uncle Perry asked, "Ethel, is there anything new? Anything that hasn't been said a dozen times before?"

She hesitated. "No, nothing new. Just a lot of talk about how much the state might pay for land or for a house, how much for a business, like the hotel in Enfield, or the box company, or the button shops, or even a charcoal kiln. Or how much timber on the stump might be worth. I can't bear to hear all this talk about selling out. There are some things, like this farm, our home, that are worth more than money." She got up and went into the parlor.

The sweet taste of honey went bitter. Josiah thought of Addy and "enemy domain," of the right to take. But, he thought, taking land isn't any fairer that Alvin taking my marbles just because he's bigger, except that taking marbles is really such a little thing and what the Commonwealth of Massachusetts might do is an enormous thing. Beyond enormous.

23
The Letter

IT WAS A COLD, RAW, AND WINDY DAY in early November, the sort of day when one realizes how early the dark settles over the land. Josiah came in from school and found Aunt Ethel sitting in the parlor, just sitting there holding a letter in her hand. She looked up as he entered the room. "It's from your Uncle Albert."

Taking a step toward her, Josiah asked eagerly, "What does it say?"

"I haven't opened it. I figure if I've been waiting all these years to get another letter from Albert, then I can wait a bit longer, until I get myself settled back down and we've eaten supper. This letter has been at the post office for the best part of a week anyway. Lucky thing Perry went into town today." She got up, placed the letter carefully on her desk, and went into the kitchen.

A letter from Uncle Albert! Now I'll find out what happened to him, Josiah thought. Maybe he's writing to say he's coming back. Maybe he'll want his old room back. If I were Aunt Ethel, I'd be tearing open that letter. He glanced at the envelope lying quietly on the desk, wishing he could grab it and read it. Instead he went out to do his chores.

It wasn't until after supper that Aunt Ethel finally did open the letter, slitting the envelope slowly with a sharp knife. There was only one folded piece of paper inside, with writing on both sides. Uncle Perry and Josiah waited impatiently while she read it to herself, her lips moving soundlessly. Then she folded it back up and slid it into its envelope. "I am relieved that he is still among the living," she announced. She didn't even have to read the letter to know that, Josiah thought. Uncle Perry cleared his throat and asked, "Well, how is your brother Albert?"

"Hard to tell, really. Here, read it for yourselves," she said, handing the letter to Uncle Perry. He opened it and read it slowly, his eyebrows going up and down a few times, and handed it on to Josiah without comment.

> Fresno, California
> October 17, 1926
>
> Dear Ethel,
>
> Your letter, sent last February, just reached me. I was saddened to hear about our sister and her husband—I always had a soft spot for her. Never met her husband, as you know. Didn't know I had a nephew, but I was glad to hear he has come to live with you on the old farm.
>
> It's been a long, long time since I wrote. I thought I'd wait until I'd made my fortune—I believed that anybody could get rich in the far west, but I've learned different.
>
> Over the years I've worked building houses and even done some farmwork, if you can imagine that, given what I said when I left home. I keep moving around from place to place, hoping I might get lucky. Sometimes I tuck Pa's old fiddle under my chin and sing and play for my supper, and sometimes people tell me I should be in the motion pictures, but I've never tried it yet.
>
> I often think of the beautiful valley I left behind. Hope this finds you and Perry well. Perhaps someday I will meet my nephew Josiah.
>
> Your brother,
> Albert

Josiah read the letter a second time, to make sure he hadn't missed anything, and then handed it to Aunt Ethel. She gave her head a funny little shake and put the letter into her apron pocket. "When I saw his writing on the envelope, I hoped he might be coming home. Should have known better," she said, as if to herself. "I'll write to him soon at this new address to tell him that we're all well."

As he lay in Uncle Albert's old bed that night, tossing because he couldn't sleep, Josiah thought about his uncle. That made him think of a poem they had read in school, one he liked. He recited the first verse:

> *Gaily bedight,*
> *A gallant knight,*

In sunshine and in shadow,
Had journeyed long
Singing a song,
In search of Eldorado

He imagined an Albert who might "Ride, boldly ride," even if the road led "Over the Mountains of the Moon, Down the Valley of the Shadow," as in Poe's poem. But it seemed as though, like that knight, his uncle had not yet found Eldorado, that mythical place of great wealth. Uncle Albert, Josiah reminded himself, is not rich or famous, he's not coming back anytime soon, and it sounds as if he doesn't really live anywhere. But, on the other hand, he does hope to meet me, perhaps.

24
Trees, Turkeys, and Bridges

The following Sunday, after almost all the harvesting was done, Uncle Perry announced that he would show Josiah how to use an ax. "But I've been using an ax to split kindling ever since last spring," Josiah protested.

"I mean up in the woodlot, chopping down trees, not in the woodshed. We'll be needing to get in more wood."

"But the woodshed's crammed full of wood, and there are cords of it stacked outside." At least now he could speak about "cords" and know that a cord meant a pile of wood that measured four feet by four feet by eight feet. There was also an enormous pile by the sugarhouse. "And Aunt Ethel told me there was more than enough to keep the kitchen stove, the parlor stove, and even the old fireplace fed all winter."

"Yes, and that's all dry wood. We'll be cutting for next year."

Of course, Josiah thought, it was all part of what his aunt called "planning ahead."

Uncle Perry carried a well-sharpened ax as they walked up into the woods over ground carpeted with fallen leaves and between trunks of oak, cherry, ash, beech, birch, and maple. Scattered among the hardwoods were patches of green-needled pines and hemlocks. Some dry leaves still clung to the branches of beeches and oaks. Josiah could identify most of the trees now by their bark and shape. Uncle Perry pointed to some sprouts rising from a stump. "Do you know what these are?" he questioned. Josiah shook his head.

"They're chestnut," he said. "Sprouts of an old chestnut tree."

"We had to learn a poem in school this week about that tree," Josiah reported. "It starts out 'Under a spreading chestnut-tree / The village smithy stands.' Mr. Richardson says that they had good nuts."

"Did he tell you that there aren't any more chestnut trees? A blight killed all of them, but it doesn't kill the roots, so they keep on sprouting, growing until the blight kills the sprouts."

"Wasn't there a way to stop the blight?" Josiah asked.

Uncle Perry shook his head. "People tried, but nothing worked. There used to be American chestnuts all through these woods, and now all we have is sprouts. Sometimes you can't stop a thing, no matter how hard you try."

Josiah nodded, thinking of how the chestnut trees were gone—and how his parents were gone. Things changed, and sometimes you couldn't stop them.

"This woodlot has some fine timber trees," Uncle Perry said, pointing to a towering white pine, its trunk rising straight to the sky. "Your grandpa always said to leave the best trees, to let them grow bigger, and then they would be worth more if we sold them for timber; nice wide boards with no knots. Course, he never believed they'd flood the valley—maybe we'll never get anything for our timber."

Uncle Perry walked over to an oak tree with a crooked trunk. "This one will never make a timber tree, only good for firewood," he remarked. Then he told Josiah to watch closely. He chopped out a notch on one side of the trunk, explaining that this would weaken the trunk, causing the tree to fall toward the notch. Next he cut on the opposite side, the swinging ax taking big bites out of the trunk. "Always make sure you're well out of the way of a falling tree."

Whack! Whack! Whack! went the ax, and Josiah saw the topmost branches start to quiver and shake. "Timber!" Uncle Perry called out, and the tree fell with a thud. Then he showed Josiah how to limb the tree, cutting off the branches and leaving the long trunk.

"Now it's time for you to try the ax," Uncle Perry said, pointing to another tree, a runty-looking one with a lean to it. "Cut your notch on the side with the lean," he added.

By now Josiah knew that things weren't always as easy as they looked. But he managed to make some chips fly, and by the time the notch was done, he felt he was getting the hang of it.

Moving around the tree a bit, he swung the ax at the trunk. Standing firm, he struck again and again, enjoying the power of his swing. The muscles in his arms and shoulders were working hard, and he wished that those boys from his old school in Boston could see him now. He wished that Addy and the Pratt boys and even Alvin could see him. It wasn't until the tree, with a sudden, snapping sound, started to fall that he realized it wasn't going to go exactly toward his notch! Jumping back, he yelled, "Timber!" as the tree came crashing down to his right.

Uncle Perry came over and looked at the stump. "Your notch is good, but you kept cutting right close to the notch, so it fell toward that cut. I knew the tree wouldn't fall on you, because it had such a lean, but next time make your main cut on the opposite side from your notch."

Examining the stump, Josiah saw the evidence of his one-sided cut. Feeling like a deflated balloon, he said, "I'll do better next time."

"Guess you will," Uncle Perry answered.

Josiah thought about how Uncle Perry let him make mistakes. Once he had overheard Uncle Perry say to Aunt Ethel, "The boy will learn best from his own mistakes. He'll remember those longer than what I tell him."

They cut a few more trees—Josiah demonstrating that he'd learned his lesson—before walking home for their Sunday dinner. They passed more chestnut sprouts, and Josiah imagined a great, spreading tree. Then he tried to imagine the whole valley underwater, with all the trees gone.

Thanksgiving was coming, and there were still the turkeys to be done. Aunt Ethel had fussed over them since last spring, ever since they were poults. Most farmers didn't bother with turkeys, and she hoped they'd bring a good price. Farming was uncertain; it wasn't like the accounting job his father had had, where you got paid every week. With farming, you could never count on making money. Was that another reason Uncle Albert left?

The turkeys were to be killed before Thanksgiving, Josiah knew, and remembering the headless hen, he hoped he wouldn't be asked to help. He wasn't. The turkeys lost their heads while Josiah was at school, and Aunt Ethel had already cleaned and plucked most of them before he got home. "Too bad these aren't geese," she said, glancing at the pile of feathers. "Then we'd have enough down to make pillows and even a new quilt.

Turkey feathers are good for nothing. Maybe next year we'll raise some geese. There's still a market for a Christmas goose."

There it is again, Josiah thought, how to make a bit of money to pay for things that you can't grow on a farm.

One turkey was kept aside, and Uncle Perry took the rest to be sold. He came back from town looking pleased and bringing a supply of tea and coffee and a jar of olives, as well as a new pair of shoes for Josiah. "You can wear them on Thanksgiving," Aunt Ethel said. "I've invited the Damons to come eat with us."

By the time that the Damons arrived on Thanksgiving Day, bringing a large dish of vegetables and some pies, the house smelled deliciously of roasting turkey. Mrs. Damon looked tired, and even Josiah could tell by looking that she was expecting.

Addy's sister Betty was all excited, telling everyone that she was quitting school and getting a real factory job in Athol, starting next week. Addy didn't seem too pleased about it, though. "Now I'll have to help Ma more, do more housework and everything," she told Josiah. "I don't see why Betty has to be in such a rush to leave the valley, even before we have to. But she says she'll give most of what she earns to Ma and Pa, so they said she could."

From across the room, Josiah and Addy heard Mr. Damon say to Aunt Ethel, "I hear you had a letter from my old pal Albert."

"It's the first we've had for a long, long while. He's in California now."

"I wonder if they dam up rivers out there," Mr. Damon said. "As I remember, he was sure that they'd do it here, dam up the Swift. He had that big fight with his pa about it, just before he left. Seems Albert was right, and that was long before the report in 1922."

"Fred, you know I don't like to talk about those reservoir plans. I'd never mention them in a letter to Albert. And as it is Thanksgiving Day, I hope we can talk of other things," Aunt Ethel replied curtly. She turned and went to the stove.

Addy grabbed Josiah's arm. "Why didn't you tell me that your Uncle Albert wrote to you?" she asked Josiah.

"He wrote to my aunt, not to me. He didn't even know I existed until now. He still has the fiddle and he plays it, but you were wrong—he's not famous. Also, he hopes to meet me."

"Well, I hope he comes back here, at least for a visit, so I can hear him play that fiddle."

Then dinner was ready, and there was no more talk of Uncle Albert or of flooding the valley. Josiah ate turkey and stuffing and vegetables and pies until he felt more than stuffed.

It wasn't until a few days later that he decided to write to Uncle Albert himself. But once he sat down with paper and pen, he found that none of the letters he had written in his head wanted to be written down. After tearing up his first attempt, he wrote a quite short letter.

> Dear Uncle Albert,
> I found your harmonica and your marbles. I hope you don't mind my having them.
> Would you tell me why you left here all those years ago?
> Do you think you will ever come back for a visit? I hope you do and please bring the fiddle.
>
> Your nephew,
> Josiah Johnson Wallace
>
> P.S. If you're coming, you'd better come soon, because they might flood the valley.

After reading over the letter, he decided that it would do, although he had never actually written a letter to anyone before, just practice exercises that he had to write in school. He folded it, and then it came over him that he didn't have an envelope or a stamp or even Uncle Albert's address in California. He didn't want to tell Aunt Ethel about his letter, but how else was he going to be able to send it?

"What do you mean you've written to your Uncle Albert? You don't even know him," Aunt Ethel exclaimed.

"I wanted to tell him about his harmonica, that's all. And I'd like to know him."

She made a noise that sounded like "hrumph," and then said, "Well, I suppose there's no harm." Shaking her head, she fetched an envelope and stamp from her desk. "He probably won't answer, so don't you go getting your hopes up." She watched as he licked the stamp and envelope flap—the glue had a nasty taste that stayed on his tongue. "You didn't say anything in your letter about me playing that harmonica, did you?" she asked.

Josiah tried to imagine Aunt Ethel as a girl who wanted to play her big brother's harmonica, but he said seriously, without even a smile, "No, ma'am, I didn't." Then he looked at the blank envelope. "Excuse me, but I need the address, too."

He heard that "hrumph" sound again as Aunt Ethel went back to her desk and returned with Uncle Albert's letter. "When you're done, give your letter to Uncle Perry and he'll take it to post next time he goes to the village or into town." She went to the stove, shook down the grates, and put in some wood.

Carefully Josiah copied out the address, wondering what California was like. That set him to thinking about where in the world they could go if they had to leave the valley. He didn't want to go back to Boston anymore. He pictured the map of the whole United States that Mr. Richardson had tacked to the schoolhouse wall. Beyond New England there was the South, but that would be too hot; or the Dakotas—his pa had had a friend who went to North Dakota and wrote back that it was "frigid with mountainous snow drifts"—or Kansas, but he'd heard it was all flat there. Then he thought of one of Aunt Ethel's sayings: "No point in crossing bridges until you come to them."

25

Snow, Pigs, and Worry

THE FIRST REAL SNOW, FOLLOWED BY COLD, ARRIVED on the last day of November—a week late, according to the Almanac. The sky had gone gray and heavy-looking in the afternoon, and by the time Josiah woke up the next morning there was over half a foot of white covering everything. They had to shovel paths to the barn, the privy, the hen house, and out to the road—it was the kind of snow that packed, not the light and fluffy kind that slides easily off snow shovels.

The sky was clearing as Josiah left for school, wearing, at Aunt Ethel's insistence, an old knit hat, a scarf, and mittens. He wondered if they had once belonged to Uncle Albert, like the still-too-big boots on his feet. The snow made for slow walking, and Addy told Leena to go last so that she could walk in the already broken trail. "The sleds and sleighs will get it packed down soon," Addy remarked to Josiah.

"In Boston the plows would be out, pushing the snow off the streets," Josiah said.

"Well, if we were in Enfield, they would have the big pungs out already, smoothing and packing the snow down for the runners on the sleighs and sleds. Why would you want to get the snow off the roads?" she asked.

"For the motorcars and trucks, of course," Josiah replied. "In the city, most people have automobiles now instead of horses, or you can take the street railway."

"Well, I'd rather ride behind a fast-trotting horse with sleigh bells. But my sister Betty, she says horses are backward and that she'll get a motorcar if ever she can."

The day at school passed slowly, with all the pupils anxiously waiting to go out for recess so that they could build snowmen and toss snowballs, and then waiting for the school day to end. At last the afternoon session was over, and Mr. Richardson rang the bell for dismissal.

Josiah was barely out of the schoolyard when a snowball hit him on the back of the head. He turned, and a second snowball, packed hard, banged into his face, smacking his nose. He wiped snow out of his eyes and saw Alvin with another snowball ready to fly. Josiah ducked and hastily grabbed some snow, flinging it at Alvin. "You call that a snowball?" Alvin taunted, brushing the snow off his chest. But Josiah's next shot hit him on the ear.

"I'm going to teach you a lesson, Boston Boy. I'm going to wash your face with snow. Don't need a reservoir to do that!" He advanced toward Josiah.

Now I will have to fight, Josiah thought as he threw more snow and missed. Alvin stepped closer. Josiah readied a snowball and aimed it at Alvin's face. He threw and didn't miss. Alvin lunged for him, nearly taking him down. Suddenly, other snowballs whizzed past, targeting Alvin. Addy and the Pratt boys were pelting Alvin with missiles, plastering him with snow.

"No fair! That's four against one," Alvin hollered. His next snowball got Josiah smack in the face. Alvin smiled, then turned his back on them and walked away.

"Alvin is big, so why does he have to be such a bully?" Tom Pratt asked. "Why can't he just mind his own business?"

"He's big, but he wants to feel bigger," Addy replied. "My pa says that's the way the Slades are. But I don't know why."

Josiah thought back to the conversation he had overheard about Mr. Slade and the strap, but he didn't say anything.

THE METROPOLITAN DISTRICT WATER SUPPLY COMMISSION had been formed, and new legislation had been proposed in Boston. Citizens in the valley attempted to organize to protect their towns. News of events reached the people of the Swift River Valley in stages, quickly in Enfield and the other town centers, slowly on outlying farms. "If we had telephones the way they do in Boston, I would have known all about this article days ago," Aunt Ethel spluttered, after reading the latest update in the newspaper.

"But, Ethel, nothing is settled yet, and just because we didn't get the newspaper until I went into town today doesn't change that," Uncle Perry replied. "They say there will be more hearings before anything is really decided."

"It's just more waiting, that's what it is."

Looking from his aunt to his uncle, Josiah couldn't make head or tail of what it all meant. Aunt Ethel read the article several times, then clipped it out and was headed for her desk when Josiah asked if he could see it.

"Here," she said. "But Uncle Perry's right, it doesn't settle anything."

Once he'd read it, Josiah had to agree. The next day at school there was some talk of the article, but none of it made anything clearer. Alvin came up to him in the schoolyard and poked a finger into Josiah's chest. "My pa says the people of Boston can die of thirst for all he cares. And I say you should go back where you came from."

"I don't care what your pa says, and I'm not leaving!" They were standing so close that Josiah felt Alvin's breath, smelled it even. He's going to hit me, Josiah thought in a flash, and I'll have to hit him back. His heart thumped and the muscles in his arms tensed. Alvin's fists went up. At that instant Mr. Richardson rang the bell. They both turned toward the sound and saw Mr. Richardson's eyes fixed on them. Slowly Josiah backed away and then headed for the door. Alvin followed him into the schoolhouse.

That was close, Josiah thought, but he felt cheated out of something—out of the chance to land at least one punch on Alvin before Alvin knocked him down.

WHEN JOSIAH GOT HOME THAT DAY, Uncle Perry told him that they would be slaughtering the pigs on Saturday. In fact, they were purposely waiting until Saturday so that Josiah would be there. The pigs had grown as round as barrels, and with the cold weather the meat would keep.

Mr. Damon came to help, and Josiah could tell that neither of the men had much stomach for the job at hand. One at a time, the pigs, all unaware, were brought up to the front of the barn, where the carcasses could be hauled up off the floor. Josiah had fed those pigs all summer and fall, and while he didn't exactly love pigs, he wished he were almost anywhere else. At the last moment he turned away, and then there was just a dead pig and he did what he was told, helping to turn the pigs into bacon, hams, ribs, chops, and sausages. One of the worst jobs was preparing and cleaning the intestines to make casings for sausages. The Damons had a smokehouse where the hams and bacon would be cured in exchange for a share of the meat. Josiah didn't think he would ever want to eat any of it.

THE COLD DESCENDED AND JOSIAH BROUGHT IN ARMLOADS OF WOOD for the hungry fires. The days grew shorter and the evenings longer. Aunt Ethel sat knitting or darning socks, close to the stove with her house cat in her lap and Shep curled nearby. Josiah did his lessons by lantern light at the kitchen table.

Before Josiah went up to bed, Aunt Ethel would hand him a brick of soapstone that had been heated on the stove and then wrapped in an old towel or piece of blanket. The soapstone, he learned, was quarried in Prescott and used for making sinks, like the one in the farmhouse kitchen, and other items. Placed under the covers at the bottom of his bed, the piece of soapstone gradually released its warmth, keeping his feet cozy at least at the start. By morning the soapstone was cold. He could see his breath in his room, and he shivered as he dressed.

It was almost Christmas when he went with Uncle Perry to a place near the bog where small fir trees grew. Josiah picked out one a head taller than he was and cut it. They brought it home and set it up in the parlor.

Aunt Ethel got an old silver-colored star out of her desk and tied red ribbon bows on the branches. Then she rubbed the kernels from small ears of popcorn, popped the corn, and strung what they didn't eat into decorations for the tree. Once it was done, she stood back, her hands on her hips, and said, "There," in a satisfied tone. Josiah's parents had never made much fuss about Christmas, and he didn't expect any presents. The tree was enough.

For their Christmas dinner, Aunt Ethel baked one of the hams with apples, and there were potatoes and onions and a sort of fruitcake. Josiah had already discovered that he couldn't resist bacon or sausage from the pigs once it was cooked and on the table. "We don't usually bother much with Christmas," Aunt Ethel said, "but since you're here, I decided we would." He felt warm all the way through, and at the same time sad, remembering his parents. Josiah saw that Aunt Ethel had mended the blue-and-white teacup that his mother had dropped when she fell ill. It sat in the center of the table, holding small sprigs of evergreen with red berries.

Then, after dinner, Aunt Ethel brought out two packages and, to his surprise, handed both to Josiah. One was a sweater that she had knit, though she must have worked on it only when he wasn't there to see. The other, he could tell, was a book. When he got the paper off, he saw that it was an old copy of *Kidnapped*—a story he had heard about but never read.

"That book belonged to your Uncle Albert. I'm sure he would want you to have it," he heard his aunt saying. "I had hoped—not expected, but hoped—that we might have a letter from him by now."

Listening to her, Josiah realized that he had more than hoped—he had expected that Uncle Albert would answer his letter right away. Perhaps his uncle didn't like his letter. "I'll read the book soon, and maybe I'll write to tell him," he said. "Thank you for the sweater," he added.

Aunt Ethel just nodded her head and said, "I think I'll brew up a pot of tea. I could use a cup."

More snow arrived before New Year's Day, but there was no letter from California. In the barn Uncle Perry chopped up mangels for the cows, and Josiah smelled the sweetness of the enormous sugar beets on the cows' breath as he milked. The warmth of the animals, of the manure pile mounting under the barn, and the insulating layers of hay piled above in the loft all kept the barn from becoming as cold as it was outside. "If this storm gets any fiercer, it will be a blizzard," Uncle Perry remarked. A gusty wind howled around the barn, whipping the fine snow into drifts. Uncle Perry worried aloud about whether the roads might be impassable in the morning and about when the milk might be picked up.

After the milking was finished, Josiah climbed the ladder to the loft and forked down hay for the cows and for Ned and Nellie. Once all the mangers were filled with hay, he went to check on Brindle, who was lying down and chewing her cud in the special stall at the end of the tie-up. He looked at her bulging sides and wondered how soon the calf would come. It was better to have calves born in spring or summer, but then all the cows would be going dry at once, so this would be a winter calf. As usual, Uncle Perry hoped for a heifer, a future milk cow.

It was 1927 now, and while Josiah was glad to see the end of 1926, it seemed that an uncertain year lay ahead. There was always something to worry about on a farm, but it was more than that. There was the dam, and the power of the government in Boston to change everything.

26
A Calf and a Geology Lesson

Wind drove the snow against Josiah's windows during the night, and he pulled the extra quilt right over his head. The snow kept coming, and there was no school for three days—at least if there was, Josiah didn't go—and the milk wasn't picked up, either.

It was on the last day of the storm, when the sky was already clearing, that Brindle decided to have her calf. Josiah watched alongside Uncle Perry as the cow heaved and kept lying down and getting up again.

"I'm going up to the house for a while," Uncle Perry announced, "so keep an eye on the cow. Brindle's had lots of calves and knows just what to do, but you call me right away if there's any trouble."

He nodded and heard Uncle Perry open and close the barn door. The only trouble, Josiah told himself, is that I'm not sure how to tell if a cow is in trouble. I've only seen one calf born, and there was no trouble at all; the calf just slipped out, the mother licked it, and it got up and found her teat.

Brindle looked tired as she turned around restlessly, lay down again, and got up again. What was taking Uncle Perry so long back at the house? The cow heaved and groaned—was that what she was supposed to do? Wait! Was that something poking out of her? Yes! It must be one of the little hooves that were meant to come out first, he thought. More heaves, but nothing happened. Where was the other hoof? What had Uncle Perry told him about calves getting stuck, about someone having to reach in and bring the hooves together, even having to push the calf back? He'd better get help.

Better check Brindle first, he thought—maybe he could do something. He rolled up his sleeve and reached out to touch the single hoof. Maybe I can just feel for the other one, so I can tell Uncle Perry what's happening, he said to himself. He closed his eyes as his hand explored above the first hoof. There, the other one was right above! His fingers closed around it, managing somehow to bring it almost even with the first hoof. Brindle strained some more, and he could see what had to be the nose of the calf, still covered by the birth sack. It would be all over in a minute, no need to call Uncle Perry.

Brindle lay down, heaving off and on, but the calf didn't slide out. Josiah started to run for Uncle Perry, but the cow moaned and he ran back, seeing the little calf still stuck, mostly in and a bit out. The cow grunted and her sides shook, but the body of the calf stayed stuck. Before Josiah knew what he was doing, he grabbed the calf's slippery legs and pulled, tugging as hard as he could. Brindle gave a great heave. The calf came out so fast that Josiah fell backwards and was left sitting with the calf in his lap.

Now Brindle was supposed to get up and come clean off the calf. It lay limp across Josiah's legs. Brindle didn't budge. The calf's not breathing, he realized; it can't breathe, because of the birth membrane. He pushed the warm, wet body of the calf off his lap and got up. The calf might die before I can get Uncle Perry, he thought, starting to panic. Reaching down, he clawed at the membrane, clearing it from the calf's nose and head. Nothing happened. "Please, please, don't die," he begged, patting its soggy coat, then rubbing it hard all over with an old burlap bag. Finally the calf took a sucking breath and then another and another. He rubbed it some more. Brindle looked around, slowly pulled herself to her feet, came over, and started licking the calf. Josiah ran for the house.

"She had the calf!" he announced, panting and full of the excitement of birth.

"Is it a heifer?" Uncle Perry asked.

"I don't know. I forgot to look."

"Well, let's go see," Aunt Ethel said, so they all went out to the barn. They arrived in time to watch the calf wobble to its feet, and Josiah saw that it was indeed a heifer. Then he told them how there was a little trouble and what he had done. Uncle Perry nodded his head and said, "Doesn't sound as though you needed me." And that, Josiah knew, was as close to praise as Uncle Perry was likely to come.

"Why, I think you saved that little calf," Aunt Ethel told him. They all watched while the calf had her first drink of milk.

"She's the prettiest little heifer I ever saw," Josiah proclaimed.

That night at supper, Uncle Perry made an announcement: "You helped to bring that calf into the world, and your aunt and I have decided that she should be yours, to start your herd. Not that it's a very good time to go into dairy farming in this valley, but she's a fine calf."

Josiah was so surprised he couldn't say anything at first, but he felt a smile growing on his face. "And since she's yours," Aunt Ethel said, "you'll have to pick out a name for her. Names are important, even for a cow."

After supper he took a lantern and went out in the snow to the barn to check on his calf. He thought about names—it seemed that many of the cows had flower names, but probably that was because Aunt Ethel liked flowers. Violet? Daffodil? Maybe Petunia? No, no, and no! Her coat, all dry and fluffy now, was a rich brown with little white spots like snowflakes. There should be a reason for her name, just the way I'm named after my grandpa, he thought. Then it came to him. Her name will be Snowflake, he decided, because of the blizzard and her markings. And when she grows up, she'll graze in the pastures that my great-grandpa first cleared. He could see a whole herd of cattle grazing peacefully and drinking at the brook.

The next day, as Josiah trudged to school, he told Addy all about his calf. "That's nice," she said. "I never had a calf, not even a kitten all my own. Maybe I can come over and see her. But," she continued, "you'll need a lot more cows for a herd. My pa says that these days you can't really make a living unless you're going to be milking more cows, maybe even twenty-four cows. And there are all the new regulations that the state says you have to follow. That's one reason he keeps talking about moving, getting out of the dairy business, at least in Massachusetts. Besides, he says cows can't graze on water."

Josiah gave her a sour look, not wanting to think about all that.

AT SCHOOL MR. RICHARDSON BEGAN BY SAYING, "Today we are all going to study geology—the geology of the Swift River Valley."

"Sir, what's geology?" someone asked.

"Can anyone tell us?"

Several hands went up, including Addy's and Josiah's, but Mr. Richardson called on Tom Pratt.

"It's about rocks, isn't it?"

"Yes, about different kinds of rocks and how they were formed."

Without raising his hand, Alvin asked, "Why do we need to know about rocks?"

"Alvin, raise your hand and wait until I call on you, or else you'll be staying after school again. Now, I'll tell you why geology should matter to all of you. Ever since I came to the valley last September, I've heard a lot of talk about building a reservoir here, about damming up the river, so I've been looking into it."

Josiah leaned forward, hoping to learn something new, something that would make sense of all those clippings and everything else. But why would the answers be in geology?

"It's because of the geology of this valley that it could make a good reservoir. What I found is that there were once high mountains here, and there were volcanoes. Does everyone know what volcanoes are?" A small boy answered, "No," so Mr. Richardson explained about how melted rock, lava, and hot rocks erupt out of volcanoes. Even Alvin seemed to be paying attention.

"In this area, all that volcanic rock got squeezed together into a kind of rock called gneiss, making great, high hills of gneiss. Then came glaciers and a long Ice Age, and the glaciers made the valleys between the hills deeper." Addy's hand went up and he called on her.

"Why did the glaciers come? Why did it get so cold?"

"I'll have to look into that some more. The scientists don't seem to agree, as far as I can tell. But what I do know is that, for whatever reason, the world started to warm up and the glaciers melted. When all that ice was gone, it left behind the Swift River Valley, with rocky hills all around the edges and some in between the East Branch and the West Branch of the river. So to make a reservoir, all they would have to do is dam up the river in two places at the lower end of the valley and the whole valley would flood."

"Sounds like you think that's a good idea. Well, I don't," Alvin interrupted. And for once Josiah felt the same way. To his surprise, Mr. Richardson just ignored the interruption.

"You see, the water of the Swift River is excellent water, filtered naturally, and the hills would hold it in and the gneiss bottom wouldn't let it all leak out. There's one more thing: this valley is higher than Boston, so the water from the reservoir would flow to the city by gravity; it wouldn't have to be pumped."

"So you think they should do it?" Alvin interrupted again.

"You will clean the blackboard after school, Alvin," Mr. Richardson said. But then he replied to Alvin's question. "No, I don't want to see this beautiful valley flooded. However, I can understand why the engineers in Boston think it would work, why a reservoir here would be able to solve their water problems."

Addy raised her hand. "I don't think it's right. Boston shouldn't be allowed to make us move, to drown our valley."

"It may not be fair, but the law says that the Commonwealth of Massachusetts does have the right to do what it thinks is best for the whole state," Mr. Richardson explained. "I've never been to Boston, but most of the people in this state live in or near Boston, so I guess the politicians are going to do what they decide is best for them, not for the people who live here."

Addy's hand waved wildly. "Maybe they don't even need more water. Josiah used to live in Boston, and he said plenty of water always came out of the faucets." Josiah stared down at the floor, wishing Addy had kept her mouth closed.

Tom Pratt was called on next. "I heard that there's lots of water closer to Boston. Why don't they use that?"

"It seems they are still considering other solutions that would cost less. We don't know what they will decide to do. Building tremendous dams and a big tunnel to take the water to Boston would be very expensive," Mr. Richardson said. "We'll have to wait and see. Now it's time for recess."

There it was again, Josiah thought, more waiting. And why couldn't Boston solve its own problems? He would never be able to have a herd of cows grazing on Grandpa Johnson's farm if they built this reservoir.

27
The Fight

Josiah stamped out of the schoolhouse and started down the steps for recess. Suddenly he was pushed from behind and went sprawling. "Too bad you slipped, Boston Boy!" Alvin jeered. "You're not going to get our water without paying for it."

Back on his feet, Josiah said, "Stop calling me 'Boston Boy.' I don't want a reservoir; just leave me alone!"

"Boston Boy! Boston Water Boy!" Alvin taunted, moving away from the schoolhouse.

Josiah came after him, his fists up. Alvin stood there like a mountain, with his hands ready. Josiah threw a punch, hitting Alvin's arm. Alvin got him on the face, smashing into Josiah's nose and eye. Josiah, his nose bleeding, slugged up at Alvin's chin. Then Alvin landed a hard one on Josiah's chest, pushing him backwards.

Another hit and Josiah was down. A crowd gathered. "Come on, Josiah! Get up!" Tom Pratt urged.

He recovered himself, rising slowly, coming at Alvin, jabbing uselessly. Josiah took a punch on his face, then he socked Alvin. Alvin landed a hard one, knocking Josiah back to the ground. He lay there for a moment, thinking that there was no way he could win, that Alvin would beat him to a pulp.

"Going to quit, Sissy?" Alvin shouted. "Quitter! Sissy, Boston Water Boy!"

"He's not a quitter!" Addy shouted back.

Josiah gathered his strength and stood up, breathing hard.

"Boston Boy's a loser!" Alvin jeered.

Josiah took a few steps back, then lowered his head and ran at Alvin like an angry bull. His head crashed into Alvin's middle. Alvin tumbled backwards onto the frozen ground, the breath knocked clean out of him.

For an instant Josiah thought he'd killed him, but then Alvin opened his eyes. "Don't you ever, ever call me 'Boston Water Boy' again!" Josiah demanded, standing over Alvin.

At that moment Mr. Richardson came leaping down the steps of the schoolhouse, calling out, "No fighting! No fighting at my school!" The pupils ringing the scene of the fight made way for him. He saw Josiah's battered face and ordered him into the schoolhouse. A few minutes later the teacher came in with Alvin.

"Now what's this all about? Alvin, what do you have to say for yourself?"

"Nothing. Josiah knocked me down, that's all."

"Josiah, what about you?"

"Alvin pushed me down the steps, and we had a fight. I told him to stop calling me 'Boston Water Boy.' I don't like it."

"Why do you call him that?" Mr. Richardson asked.

"Because he comes from Boston, and they want our water, like you said."

"I see," said Mr. Richardson, although Josiah doubted that he did. "If I catch either of you fighting again, or causing any other trouble, you will be expelled from this school. Do you understand?"

"You mean I wouldn't have to come to school anymore?" Alvin asked. "That wouldn't be so bad."

Mr. Richardson stared at Alvin. "I will send a letter home with you today, telling what you just said, and exactly what will happen if there is any more trouble. And I will ask for a reply."

"Don't do that!" Alvin exclaimed. "I didn't mean it about not coming to school. If you tell my pa, he'll whip me again, something terrible. Please don't send a letter," Alvin begged.

Josiah watched as Alvin seemed to come all to pieces, and he thought back to what he'd overheard Aunt Ethel say when he was on the stairs, about a strap.

28

Cutting Ice and Another Letter

By the time Mr. Richardson rang the last bell, Josiah's eye was swollen shut. Alvin stayed behind in the schoolhouse to clean the blackboard as the others filed out. Josiah soon found himself surrounded by his fellow pupils, as if he were some sort of hero. Part of it felt right—he was almost strutting like a rooster—but part of it didn't. He kept thinking about Mr. Slade whipping Alvin, and wondering if he used a real whip or hit Alvin with a belt or what.

Walking home with Addy and the Pratt boys, he felt relieved more than anything else, as if he had taken a hard test and, to his surprise, passed with an A.

"You sure let him have it," Tom said admiringly.

"All I really did was knock Alvin over; he was winning before that. Probably anybody could have done it."

"No," said Addy. "Besides, nobody else did it. I wish I'd at least done something when Alvin yanked my braids this morning."

Josiah was about to tell them about Alvin being whipped when Addy continued: "Alvin isn't fair about anything. It serves him right, for a change. And if they do flood the valley, we're all in this together—Josiah as much as the rest of us." She turned to Josiah. "Even if you did come from Boston, your ma didn't, and you're here now."

The Pratt boys both nodded agreement, and Tom said, "My granny's real worried that they're going to build that dam, and after what Mr. Richardson said today, so am I."

When Josiah got home, Aunt Ethel took one look at him and scrunched her mouth into a hard line. "Remind me of your Uncle Albert, you do. He used to come home looking like that—black eyes and bloody noses. Albert would fight with Ira Slade most times—hard to know who won. And that uncle of yours still hasn't answered our letters." She turned away, her hand over her eyes.

After a moment Josiah went to the barn, to see Snowflake. He guessed that a calf couldn't know enough to worry about much of anything; she looked so peaceful and contented, full of milk. He chewed on a hay stem and thought how strange it was that he could find comfort in a calf.

As he lay in bed that night, he began thinking about the fights that Uncle Albert had had with Alvin's pa—lots of fights, and it was hard to say who won, Aunt Ethel had said. Maybe Uncle Albert had been good at fighting, an even match for Mr. Slade. But Josiah knew he probably wouldn't be lucky enough to win another fight against Alvin. Perhaps Alvin would ambush him on the way to or from school or somewhere else. Well, he thought, tomorrow is Saturday, so I won't see Alvin. We're going to go cut ice on the pond.

JOSIAH AND UNCLE PERRY HURRIED THROUGH MORNING CHORES and breakfast, then harnessed Nellie up to the big sled, loaded on an ice saw and ice tongs, and set off. Other men and boys, horses and sleds, were there before them, starting to harvest the thick ice. There was talk about a team with a loaded sled that fell through on Quabbin Lake, over in Greenwich. "They should have waited—the ice wasn't strong enough to hold—and what a time they had getting the horses out. Lucky it was so near the shore." Someone else told about the man who built a giant icehouse by Greenwich Lake over the summer. "Guess he plans to sell a lot of ice. Figures that dam's not coming anytime soon, if ever."

Suddenly Josiah saw Alvin and his pa sawing ice into square blocks. Why hadn't he thought that Alvin might be here, that there might be trouble? Watching, he could tell that Alvin knew just how to cut ice and haul the big chunks out of the water. He saw that Alvin was working hard—he didn't seem like the Alvin at school who almost never knew his lessons.

Later, as they were loading ice onto the sled, he saw Alvin looking at him, but neither of them said anything. The way Alvin lifted the big chunks made it look as if they were made of feathers. Would Alvin knock him into the freezing water if he got the chance, pretending it was an accident? Josiah pushed that thought out of his head as he struggled to get another block onto the sled. They took their first load home and piled the blocks onto the sawdust-covered floor of the icehouse, then went back for another load. It reminded Josiah of filling the barn with hay, load after load; hay cut in summer for the long, cold winter, and ice cut in winter for the long, hot summer.

They cut more ice the next day, and the Slades were there again, but working on the other side of the cutting area. On Monday it was back to school. When Josiah and Alvin saw each other, they both acted as if nothing had happened, as if there hadn't been a fight. But once during the day, Josiah caught Alvin looking at him. *If he calls me "Boston Boy" even one more time, then it's not over,* Josiah thought. Still, there was no ambush on the way home.

As soon as Josiah came into the house, into the kitchen, he could tell that Aunt Ethel was agitated, upset about something. "Uncle Perry went into town today," she said. Then she went into the parlor, to her desk, and came back holding an envelope. "Here," she said, thrusting the envelope at him. "It's addressed to you—a letter from Albert."

Startled, he took a moment to reach for it, then tore the envelope open and unfolded the single sheet of paper inside. He was aware of his aunt standing stock-still, her eyes on the letter, waiting.

> *Dear Nephew,*
> *You go right ahead and play with that harmonica and the marbles.*
>
> *Why did I leave home? Well, I hated being told what to do—by the rooster when he crowed every morning, by the cows, by the hay, by the maple sap, by the weather, and, of course, by your grandpa and grandma. You don't own a farm, a farm owns you! It tells you when to work and decides how you'll get paid. Remember that.*
>
> *Also, I was sure they'd flood the valley sooner or later. I thought sooner, but my pa wouldn't listen. We had a big argument and I left.*

> *I'm in a place called Hollywood now. I play the fiddle every night at a restaurant. If I ever do come back, I'll bring the fiddle.*
> Your uncle, Albert

Josiah read the letter three times before he handed it over to Aunt Ethel. When she finished, she said, "Well, I never. Imagine him saying that about our parents. But then, he never did like chores, and as he was the only boy, I guess they expected more of him. I doubt I'll ever see him again."

"He might come," Josiah said. "Do you know where Hollywood is in California?"

"No. Never heard of it. Probably some no-account place." She handed the letter back to Josiah with a "hrumph," and went into the kitchen.

29
Skidding Logs and Josiah Writes

Once the icehouse was full and the ice was covered with a last load of sawdust from the sawmill, Uncle Perry said it was time to get firewood cut. Josiah thought of Uncle Albert's letter, of how on a farm something always told you what to do. This time it was the shrinking woodpiles.

Snow crunched under Nellie's spiked winter horseshoes, made to keep her from slipping on icy patches, as they reached the woodlot. After wandering around for several minutes, looking trees up and down, Uncle Perry selected a midsized, leaning oak. "It's good to have someone to put on the other end of this saw," Uncle Perry remarked. "Can't use a two-man crosscut with only one man. Now, where are we going to cut the notch?"

"The tree already has a lean on it, so it will want to fall the way it's leaning, right?"

"Yup."

"So we cut the notch here, to help it fall this way."

"Yup. Guess you've learned how to use your head," said Uncle Perry. "Let's get to work."

Josiah grasped the handles at one end of the long saw and had all he could do to keep up with Uncle Perry's push and pull from the other end. They got the notch cut quickly, and soon the cut from the back was almost through and the tree began to shiver. "Timber!" Josiah called out.

Once they had sawn off the top of the tree and limbed off the branches, Uncle Perry got Big Nellie and hooked one end of a heavy chain to the whiffletree behind her and the other around the end of a log. He gave the mare a slap on the rump and she set off, pulling the log down the hill.

"Where's Nellie going all by herself?" Josiah exclaimed.

"Skidding the log down. She knows the way home as well as you do, maybe better. But you've got to follow her down now to unhook the chain, since she can't do that, and then give her a slap to send her back. I'll pick out the next tree and have the notch chopped out by the time you get back up here."

They had a whole pile of logs in the barnyard before it was time for the afternoon milking. Josiah was feeling pleased with the day's work. "Of course," Uncle Perry reminded him, "that wood will warm us a few more times before we burn it: when we cut it into lengths, when we split it, and when we stack it." All that work just to stay warm and feed the kitchen stove, Josiah mused.

At school Alvin and Josiah had what Josiah thought of as a truce, and they avoided each other if possible. Addy wasn't asking so many questions—almost as if she didn't have the energy to be so curious now that she was responsible for all of Betty's old chores and some of her ma's as well, since Mrs. Damon had slowed down, waiting for the baby. The days were perceptibly longer, but Aunt Ethel said that the Almanac was wrong again. It had promised a thaw almost two weeks ago, and cold, gray days were following one after the other like sheep.

When the thaw came, it arrived in the middle of the night, and Josiah woke to the sound of icicles dripping outside his window. By noon the mild temperatures and the warm sunshine made the boys take off their jackets during the lunch recess. Everybody talked as if spring would arrive tomorrow.

Alvin wasn't at school that day or the next day either, but he reappeared the following morning, along with the return of freezing temperatures. He slunk into his seat, looking sullen and uncomfortable. "Glad to see you back, Alvin," Mr. Richardson said.

"I, um, ah, I fell out of the hayloft and hurt my back. That's why I missed school."

"I see," the teacher responded. "You will stay in for recess to go over what you missed." Then he returned to the morning lessons.

I bet he skipped school and spent the day out hunting or something, the weather was so nice, Josiah speculated. Then his pa found out and whipped him.

On their way home that day, after they watched Alvin limp up the drive toward the Slades' farm, Josiah told Addy and the Pratt boys what Alvin had said about getting whipped by his pa. "Perhaps that's what's wrong with his back," he finished.

"I never thought I'd hear you almost defending Alvin," Addy said. "Mr. Richardson wouldn't like whipping any better than fighting, I'd guess. Perhaps he said something to Alvin at recess, not that he could do anything. Besides, maybe Alvin did fall out of the loft."

"Doesn't a father have a right to whip his son?" Tom asked. "Not that my pa ever did, exactly, but more than once he said he would if I didn't do my chores better."

"Girls don't get whipped much, so I don't know," Addy said. "Anyway, even if his pa does take the strap to him, Alvin doesn't have to be so mean. Although, come to think of it, he hasn't pulled my braids or called me 'Carrot Head' since that fight with Josiah."

At supper that night, Uncle Perry talked about the upcoming sugaring season. He talked about how soon the weather might be right, how much syrup they might make, and even which tree gave the sweetest sap. Josiah began to think seriously about how good maple syrup tasted and about sugaring. Everyone knew it was a lot of hard work. All Josiah really remembered about last year was that Uncle Perry had made him help a few times and that a full bucket of sap was too heavy for him to carry without spilling. Uncle Perry had given up on him quickly, and at the time he was glad of it.

"Maybe this year you could set more taps, because I think I can help gather, even stay up all night boiling," he suggested.

His aunt and uncle looked at each other and then at him. "I guess with you here to give us a hand we could do that, even run a new tap line along the east side of the pasture—some good young maples there," Uncle Perry said.

"That would mean more syrup, so I could make those maple candies that the summer people buy," Aunt Ethel added.

"We'd better start fixing those old buckets I've put aside and make sure we have enough covers and spiles," Uncle Perry said, almost sounding excited. It was all Josiah could do to not let his own excitement pop out all over himself like a rash. He wondered what the old Josiah, the Josiah who, last sugaring season, was glad to be sent off to bed while the fires burned bright in the sugarhouse, would make of this.

"We'll take a look at those young maples tomorrow if we have a chance, and check out those old buckets," Uncle Perry told him.

Of course, Josiah thought, Uncle Perry wouldn't waste money on new buckets when he could repair some old ones. And in his mind he could hear Aunt Ethel saying: "Use it up, wear it out, make it do, or do without." That old saying seemed to apply to almost everything on the farm.

Later that evening, Josiah sat in his ma's rocker and read another chapter of *Kidnapped*. He was enjoying Davie's adventures and hoped the story would have a good ending. Reading the book made him think of Uncle Albert, and he decided to answer his uncle's letter. At school he had looked for Hollywood on the wall map, but he couldn't find it anywhere. The address on Uncle Albert's letter said Los Angeles, and he found that—a dot on the map in the southern part of California. Mr. Richardson told him that they didn't ever have winter there.

He got a pencil and paper and began to write:

Dear Uncle Albert,
    Thank you for answering my questions.
    I forgot to tell you that I used your fishing pole and caught some fish. I didn't break it or anything. Everything is still frozen here, so I can't go fishing again until spring.
    Aunt Ethel gave me your old book, Kidnapped. Did you have any adventures while you were going West?
    About farming, I didn't like it when I got here, but I do now. Also, Uncle Perry and Aunt Ethel gave me a little heifer to start a herd. I named her Snowflake and she's growing fast.
    Another thing, you're not a farmer, but you aren't rich and famous either. I thought when you are grown up, people stop telling you what to do, but I can see that farms don't.

Aunt Ethel told me you used to fight with Ira Slade. I had a fight with Alvin Slade.

About the dam and flooding the valley to make a reservoir for Boston. They are supposed to decide very soon. Most people think they'll do it, and then we'll have to move.

Aunt Ethel says you won't come, but I hope you will.

Your nephew, Josiah

He read over his letter and decided to take out the part about Uncle Albert not being rich and famous, and then copy the letter in ink. Writing the letter had made him wonder, though, what he would want to do if they had to leave the farm. Maybe he wouldn't want to be a farmer somewhere else.

30

A Year, Sugaring, and Brave Addy

It had been almost a year since his parents had died so unexpectedly—almost a year since he had come to the farm. Josiah got his parents' wedding picture out of the drawer and looked at them. There was that funny feeling in his throat, as if he were starting to choke, but it passed. He decided he would keep the picture out, and he set it up on top of his chest of drawers.

The notebook with all his drawings in it and the one with notes about farming were lying there, next to the picture. Soon he'd be learning about making maple syrup and about anything he hadn't paid attention to all last year, when he didn't know anything. So much had changed.

At last Uncle Perry declared that the weather was right to start sugaring. Josiah harnessed Nellie to a sled and loaded on wooden sap buckets. They set out for the sugar bush; the mare's big hooves, followed by the sled, packed down the snow.

"Why do they call a line of sugar maple trees a bush?" Josiah asked.

"It's what it's called, that's all. A sugar bush."

Nellie came to a halt at the first big maple tree, and Josiah learned how to use the bit and brace to drill a hole through the bark and into the sapwood of the tree. Then he pounded a spile—a hollow wooden spout—into the hole, hung a bucket on the spile, and put a wooden cover on the bucket. "If the temperature drops down well below freezing tonight and gets well above during the day tomorrow, we'll have a good sap run to start the season," Uncle Perry remarked.

"What if it doesn't warm up during the day?"

"Well, then the sap will stay down in the roots instead of coming up the trunk on its way to the branches, and the buckets will stay empty. You can only catch sap when it's rising."

On the big trees, they drilled for four taps, even six. The smaller ones got two or three. "Some people put more, but your Grandpa Johnson always said not to ask too much of a tree." Young trees being tapped for the first time or so only got one tap.

The next day, the weather was "right" and sap dripped into the buckets all day. After milking, they gathered the sap. Most of the buckets were at least half full, and Josiah could feel the strength in his arms as he carried the sap to the large holding tank on the sled and dumped it in. Uncle Perry used a sap yoke so that he could carry four buckets at once—two suspended from the yoke across his shoulders and one in each hand. Nellie waited patiently, knowing just where to make the next stop. "Not a real big run, but not bad for a start. We'll gather again tomorrow and then boil first thing on Saturday."

At school everybody was talking about sugaring, how many taps and when they would be boiling. The Damons didn't have a sugarhouse, but the Pratts did and so did the Slades. "My pa got a man from Enfield to come up and help us, so we'll be making the most syrup, the best syrup," Alvin boasted. "And we won't send any of it to Boston," he added, looking at Josiah. But Alvin still hadn't called him "Boston Boy" since the fight.

By the time they finished gathering sap the next day, Josiah was tired, his arms and shoulders aching from carrying almost full buckets. The following morning Uncle Perry got the fire going at full tilt under a big, rectangular, sap-filled pan, and steam began to rise from the boiling sap and drift up and out the big opening in the main roof of the sugarhouse. Soon the steam billowed out below the small, raised roof that topped the opening. A tantalizing maple smell filled the air as Uncle Perry checked and skimmed the bubbling sap. "How much longer does it have to boil?" Josiah asked as he helped stoke the fire.

"Well, figure it takes about forty gallons of sap to make one gallon of syrup, so that's a lot of boiling. We have to watch it real careful at the end, or the syrup can burn in the pan. Your aunt's the best at knowing just when it's ready."

Aunt Ethel came in and eyed the pan, then took a long-handled spoon to test the feel. "It's like making jelly. You get a sense for it," she said. At last the amber syrup was strained and ladled into jugs and jars—and at last Josiah got to taste. Yes, it was worth it.

The sugar season lasted for the next couple of weeks, off and on. Sometimes Mr. Damon came to help, and after they had a real run, with buckets overflowing everywhere, they boiled through the night. Mr. Richardson said that anyone who stayed up boiling didn't have to come to school the next day, so Josiah went to bed for a bit after the morning milking.

Addy came on a Saturday with her ma and sisters. Aunt Ethel made donuts and gave them all sugar on snow, heating some of the new syrup on the stove and pouring it over plates spread with clean snow, where the syrup became sticky candy. After Josiah's first plateful, she gave him a big sour pickle. "Here, the pickle will cut the sweet. Then you can have more."

"That's like life," Addy said. "If you get sweets, then you get pickles to take away the sweet taste."

Mrs. Damon sat heavily on one of the kitchen chairs. "I figure it could be anytime now," she said to Aunt Ethel. "I'll be glad to have it over."

"She's talking about the baby," Addy whispered to Josiah, as if he couldn't figure it out for himself. "She says she's worn and tired, so she hopes it will be easy, not like me. I guess I wasn't easy." Josiah couldn't help thinking of Brindle and wondering how it was for people. Surely they didn't get up and down and heave.

Suddenly the sugaring season was over, the snow was almost gone, and the road had turned to mud. There was mud almost everywhere as the frost came out of the ground, leaving ooze behind.

Josiah had finished reading *Kidnapped* and borrowed a copy of *The Swiss Family Robinson* from Mr. Richardson. It was slow going at first, but he kept at it and it got better. He kept the lantern burning late, wanting to see what happened next, but finally went up to bed.

He was awakened in the middle of the night by a knocking, banging sound downstairs. He ran down and got to the door just as Aunt Ethel was opening it.

Addy was standing on the doorstep, out of breath, mud all over her shoes and splashed up on her skirt. "You have to come right away! Ma needs you. She's had the baby!"

"Yes, Yes. I'll come," Aunt Ethel said, calling for Uncle Perry in the same breath.

"Pa left a while back to get the doctor, but the baby wasn't waiting. If the doctor insisted on his car, I suppose it's stuck in the mud again, and they're trying to get it out."

"Is your ma well, and the baby?" Aunt Ethel asked as she put on her coat. Addy nodded. They went out to the barn, where Uncle Perry was hooking Nellie up to a wagon by lantern light. Soon they were at the Damons' house, and Aunt Ethel rushed to Mrs. Damon's side. She was lying on a bed in a downstairs room, the one they sometimes called the birthing room.

Josiah hung back. "Where's the baby?" he asked Addy. "Did you put it in a cradle somewhere?"

"No, Ma's holding it. She won't let go of it. I had to help her, because nobody else was here." Josiah thought of how Snowflake was born. Could it have been like that?

"But I didn't tell you the most exciting part," Addy said.

What was that? Josiah wondered. Maybe when the baby started to breathe; that was the best part with Snowflake.

"The baby is a boy! Imagine! I looked the first instant he came out, and I could tell it wasn't a girl. Ma's so pleased—that's why she's still holding him. Pa will be pleased, too, when he gets here," she added, a little sadly, and Josiah remembered how she had told him that her pa taught her to fish because there weren't any boys, and now there was a boy. Maybe that part wasn't quite fair; the pickle to go with the sugar on snow.

They could hear Mrs. Damon say to Aunt Ethel, "I don't know how I would have managed without Addy. I told her to tie the extra bedsheets to the bottom bedposts, and I held them when the pains came. Next thing I knew, the baby popped out like the cork out of a bottle. There was the cord, of course, but Addy had boiling water ready and she got me the sharp shears, so I took care of that. Then she washed him a bit and wrapped him up. Isn't he beautiful?"

Almost an hour later Mr. Damon and the doctor arrived, both covered in mud. It seemed the doctor's auto got stuck in the mud and then the wagon got stuck for a bit trying to pull the auto out. That was all forgotten in the excitement of learning that it was a boy, a boy at last. The baby was held up and shown off. Josiah thought it looked sort of like a piglet, not beautiful at all, and not nearly as nice as Snowflake.

31
Spring and Opportunities

Some boston politicians and committee members came to see the Swift River and the site of the proposed dam. They ate lunch in Enfield but left the same day, and nothing was any clearer to folks in the valley than before. "Why did they bother to come all that way and not even tell us anything?" Aunt Ethel asked Uncle Perry, as if he could provide the answer.

now the ice was out on all the lakes and ponds, and clear water sparkled in spring sunshine. It was time to manure the fields, clearing the winter's accumulation out from under the barn as they shoveled load after load of manure onto the spreader. Next the fields would be plowed, turning the manure under, then harrowed, and finally the corn and other crops would be planted. Soon the blackflies were biting man and beast, looking for blood. They crawled up Josiah's pant legs, into his ears, and even into his mouth, where he couldn't help swallowing them.

Honeybees created a constant buzz in the orchard, pollinating all the blossoms and crowding in and out of the doorways of the hives, heavy with pollen. Walking past the beehives one morning as he was leaving for school, Josiah saw a great number of bees flying up out of one of the hives toward a tree branch hanging above. A tawny ball of bees clung to the branch, like a great, furry fruit. A swarm!

The ball was growing by the minute, and Uncle Perry had just left for an early trip into town. The whole swarm might fly away, with the new queen in the middle of it, and go wild if the bees weren't hived at once. He remembered Uncle Perry telling him about that, but how did you hive a swarm? He sprinted back to the house and found Aunt Ethel. "Not a swarm, not with Perry gone! Well, we'll have to manage. Usually

Uncle Perry keeps an empty hive ready, so go find it and open the cover. I'll get you the bee hat and gloves. Then you'll have to get the swarm into the hive."

Josiah dashed back to the hives, found the vacant one, and took off its cover. But how would he get the bees down? He eyed the branch. It was small and already drooped a bit with the weight of the bees. He ran to the barn and came back with a stepladder and a pruning saw. But why, he wondered, does Aunt Ethel want me to hive the swarm? Usually she can do most everything. After she gave him the hat and gloves, she just stood there, gazing toward the mass of bees from a distance. Maybe she wants to see if I can do it, Josiah thought as he put on the bee hat, tucked the veil into his shirt collar, and donned the gloves. I guess I'm on my own.

After positioning the ladder, he started climbing, hoping that what Uncle Perry had said about swarms being too busy to sting much was true. Could drones, those generally useless males, sting? He couldn't remember, but the worker bees in the swarm certainly had stingers. Carefully, about a yard away from the swarm, he held the branch with one hand and started sawing it with the other. The branch was heavier than he'd thought it would be, and he nearly dropped it as the saw cut through.

I mustn't do anything to frighten the bees, he said to himself. Nothing sudden. He almost missed the bottom step of the ladder, but his foot found it before there was a disaster. He carried the bee branch to the new hive, but it wouldn't fit inside, so he laid it across the top, leaving the swarm part in, part out. Now what? He looked to the still-distant Aunt Ethel for help, but she just waved.

Very gently, he touched the vibrating mass. The bees didn't seem to mind, although some of them crawled over his glove. He pushed the buzzing ball down, and slowly it sank into the hive until he could feel the branch through his glove. He set the cover over the bees and pulled out the branch, the cover dropping into place. It was only as he started breathing normally again that he realized a few bees had stung him on his exposed wrists.

He backed away from the hive and then turned to Aunt Ethel. "Bee stings make me swell up something terrible," she explained. "That's why Uncle Perry always looks after the bees. It's a lucky thing you were here."

"Glad to help," Josiah responded, glad to know why she couldn't help.

"Uncle Perry will be surprised," Aunt Ethel said. "Do you know the old rhyme?" Josiah shook his head. "It goes like this: 'A swarm of bees in May is worth a load of hay. A swarm of bees in June is worth a silver spoon. But a swarm of bees in July is not worth a fly.'"

Josiah was putting the ladder back in the barn when it suddenly came to him that he would be late for school. He ran most of the way, thinking of how bees didn't seem to mind moving, being relocated, but he was still quite late.

"Josiah, I'm surprised to see you tardy," Mr. Richardson said. "Do you have any excuse?"

"Yes, sir. Our bees swarmed and my uncle was away from the farm, so I had to hive them."

"I see. But stay in at recess to go over the lesson you missed."

"Yes, sir," Josiah answered, thinking that he couldn't have missed very much.

At recess Mr. Richardson told Josiah about the morning lesson. "We talked about geography. I asked the older pupils to write down three places in this country where they would like to live, if they could chose. Think about why you would want to live there. Also, be prepared to identify your choices on the map."

"Yes, sir," Josiah responded, glancing at the big wall map of the United States. It was not a new map and there was a tear at the bottom. He wondered if Mr. Richardson was glad to have moved here from Vermont. Were the bees glad to be in their new hive, right near the old one, or would they rather have flown far away?

"We'll discuss the choices after lunch."

"Anything more, sir?" Josiah asked, rubbing the bee stings on his wrist.

"That's all." Suddenly Mr. Richardson said, "Hold out your arm." Cautiously, Josiah stuck out an arm, the shirtsleeve pulling back and exposing even more of his wrist. Was the teacher going to hit him with a ruler or something for being tardy? He'd always heard that teachers did that.

"I see some of the bees got you, not that I doubted your excuse. Cold water from the pump will make the stings feel better. We kept bees on the farm where I grew up. You may go out now."

Walking down the schoolhouse steps, Josiah thought of Alvin's excuse, saying that he fell out of the loft. That was one of those excuses it was easy to doubt. A lame excuse. He nearly bumped into Alvin, who was standing at the bottom of the steps. Their eyes met.

"Hello, Josiah," Alvin said.

"What did you say?" Josiah couldn't quite believe his ears.

"I called you Josiah. Want to make something of it?" Alvin answered, his face changing.

"No, I don't," Josiah answered. "Hello, Alvin," he added rather stiffly. Was it really over? Could so much trouble fizzle down to so little, just like that?

After the lunch recess, Mr. Richardson asked for the geography choices to be handed in, and a while later he called the geography class to the front of the room. "One of your choices surprised me—several of you put down staying right here, in the Swift River Valley, at the top of your lists. The other choices were all over the map, from nearby places to Florida and California, even big cities like New York. Nobody put Boston, though."

Josiah considered his own choices: (1) stay here; (2) California, because of Uncle Albert; and (3) anywhere in New Mexico, because it sounded like adventure. He would have put Alaska for the adventure, but he thought it might be too cold.

"Can someone who chose to stay in the Swift River Valley tell me why?" Mr. Richardson inquired. Several hands went up, and Addy's got the nod. "Because it's home, that's why—and because we're probably moving to New Hampshire, dam or no dam, my pa says. Sometimes you just want what you can't have."

Nobody said much on the way home from school that day. Maybe, Josiah thought, Mr. Richardson got us all thinking and wondering about the future, about moving, about where we might go and what we might do, but we're not ready to talk about it. He decided to write another letter to his uncle, asking about life in California.

As he came up the road to the farm, he saw old Ned and Nellie standing in the pasture, so he knew that Uncle Perry was home. Shep bounded out to greet him, tail wagging.

"Go on out and find Uncle Perry," Aunt Ethel said as soon as he came into the hot kitchen. But before he went, she gave him a cool glass of fresh buttermilk and a slice of bread, spread with butter and honey. "The honey is because of this morning, because of the swarm," she told him, smiling.

He found Uncle Perry out by the bees. "I hear you got a fine, big swarm into this empty hive. I've been listening to them. We'll let them finish settling overnight and then see about putting a super in there for them to start filling. Now, your Aunt Ethel tells me that I owe you somewhat more than a load of hay but less than a silver spoon. Don't know how we'll arrange that, but it's a good thing you spotted the swarm, or those bees would be gone by now."

"I don't need hay, except for Snowflake to eat, and I don't need spoons, but I sure do like honey," Josiah replied, the taste of the honey on Aunt Ethel's bread still in his mouth. "But I would like to know why a swarm in July isn't worth anything."

"It's because if they don't start a new colony until into the summer, the bees won't have time to make enough honey to get them through the winter. Same with people—you've got to be careful when you move."

Next they got the milking done, and Josiah spent a few minutes scratching Snowflake's head between where her horns would grow. Daisy was due to calve anytime and Bessie soon after.

When they had finished supper, with rhubarb sauce for dessert, Uncle Perry started searching his pockets. "I clean forgot. There's a letter here somewhere—from Albert for Josiah." After patting all his pockets, he excused himself, and Josiah could hear him rummaging in the downstairs bedroom. He emerged a moment later, waving the letter. "Found it in the pocket of the shirt I wore to town. Here," he said, giving the envelope to Josiah.

Hollywood, California

Dear Nephew,
 Glad to know that fish are still biting in the valley. How about the blackflies?
 Do you know, I never had a calf of my own. Too late now. Good luck with yours.

About fighting—Ira Slade and I got into a lot of trouble over fights. Finally we just quit, not that we ever became real friends, but we stopped being enemies.

A man here heard me play the fiddle and sing a bit at the restaurant. He wants to make a recording of me—a record to play on a Victrola. I don't suppose you have one of those on the farm. Maybe my lucky star is about to shine.

Tell your aunt that if I make enough money from this recording to buy a train ticket, then I'll come home for a visit, and meet my nephew.

Your uncle, Albert

32
The Certainty

"I can't see as how Albert would ever make enough money from the Victrola to buy a ticket. It's just another way of saying he's not coming," Aunt Ethel insisted after she had read the letter over and over. "But if he ever is on the Victrola, then I would like to hear him. I hope he'll let us know."

"It probably takes a long time to make a recording, so we wouldn't be hearing anytime soon," Josiah remarked, feeling his aunt's disappointment. "I have to memorize a poem to recite on the last day of school," he told her, wanting to change the subject. "Mr. Richardson wants all the pupils to take part."

"That's nice."

"I chose one called 'The Road Not Taken,'" he said, thinking of the lines that reminded him of Uncle Albert: "Yet knowing how way leads on to way, / I doubted if I should ever come back." It wouldn't do any good to recite those lines to Aunt Ethel, he realized. It would only make things worse.

THERE WASN'T MUCH LEFT OF SCHOOL, only two weeks, with the final exercises in early June this year. Walking to school the next day, all Addy talked about at first was the baby, who was named Arthur James, after his two grandfathers. "He cries so hard in the middle of the night that Ma is even more tired than before. None of the girl babies was ever this much trouble," she said. Next she told him something, to Josiah's way of thinking, far more important. "Last evening Pa got back from visiting his brother in New Hampshire. Now he says that we won't move there after all, probably just stay put here for another year, until Arthur James is bigger and Ma's up to a move. So that's the good news, at least it might be."

"Sounds like good news to me," Josiah told her, and they both smiled. When the Pratt boys joined them, Nat was practicing his poem.

"That was nice," Addy said. "Want to hear mine?" And without waiting for an answer, she began to recite her whole poem, a short one by a lady named Emily Dickinson, from nearby Amherst. It began: "We never know how high we are / Till we are asked to rise."

Tom Pratt replied with:

> By the rude bridge that arched the flood,
> Their flag to April's breeze unfurled,
> Here once the embattled farmers stood
> And fired the shot heard round the world.

"That's all I can remember. Besides, I don't like the rest of it, only the part about embattled farmers," he added.

They'd all read that poem, and Josiah agreed with Tom about the rest of it. But those embattled farmers at least got to fight for their freedom, while the farmers of the Swift River Valley didn't stand a chance. There was no way he could see to have a revolution against Boston. Mr. Richardson said a man from the valley, Daniel Shays, once tried, but his rebellion was put down.

On the way home, Josiah mentioned to Addy that his Uncle Albert had sent another letter, and that someone wanted to make a recording of him playing the fiddle and singing. "Oh," she exclaimed. "Wouldn't that be exciting! We could hear him on a Victrola, and maybe he will be rich and famous after all, just the way I said."

"I doubt it," Josiah answered, but he wondered. Could his uncle have found Eldorado after all?

It was in the next week that the news finally came. The politicians had voted in Boston to pass the Swift River Act. They decided that the future water supply for the city of Boston would come from an enormous reservoir to be constructed by damming the Swift River. An office would be set up in Enfield soon, and they would begin the process of taking the land.

It's not just that the handwriting is on the wall, Josiah thought. Now we have to face the reality. Sooner or later we'll have to move—move from this place where I belong. Aunt Ethel won't talk about it, and Uncle Perry wears a frown from morning to night. Two new heifers born, and Uncle Perry doesn't even seem to care.

Was it worse for them because they had been tied to this land for so long? Josiah wasn't sure. Maybe they just couldn't imagine being anywhere else—he'd felt that way when he left Boston. He almost wished he hadn't let himself come to care about this farm, but he did care. Even so, he might be able to fit in somewhere else, and Aunt Ethel and Uncle Perry might not. They weren't old like Granny Pratt, but the older a plant is, the deeper its roots go, and the harder it is to transplant.

Josiah watched Snowflake graze in the calf pasture, and knew that he would never see his imagined herd spread across these fields. The certainty of it was terrible, like an enormous weight crushing him and everybody around him.

Walking to school, they all talked about it together, even Alvin—about the taking. It seemed that a few people still thought the reservoir might not happen, and nearly everybody agreed that it would be a while, years maybe. They wouldn't have to move right away; nothing would change overnight—except, Josiah thought, everything already had changed.

Right before the last day of school, there was another sort of news, a letter from Uncle Albert, addressed to his sister. Josiah saw that Aunt Ethel's hands were shaking as she opened it, and then her face went white. "I don't believe it," she said. "I can't believe it. Albert says he's bought a train ticket. He's coming!"

"Here, you read it," she said, thrusting the letter at Josiah before sinking onto one of the kitchen chairs and fanning herself with the envelope.

Dear Ethel,

I've made enough money from my playing and singing to pay for a round-trip ticket home. Will be arriving in about ten days.

I always said they would flood the valley, even said I wouldn't care if they did, and I remember I told Pa I hoped they would. I was angry then, but now I hope they won't. I want to see the old place again.

> *I also want to meet my nephew. He writes good letters, and they made me think hard about the home I left behind. Tell Josiah that I'll be bringing the fiddle, and I'll play all the old songs for you, along with some new ones I've learned. Don't know exactly how long I'll stay.*
>
> *From your brother, Albert*

Josiah's thoughts started jumping like corn in a popper. Now I'll get to ask Uncle Albert all the questions I want. I'll get him to tell me about his travels and California. Maybe he'll show me his Indian arrowheads and even help me find one. Maybe we can go fishing together. I'll have to tell Addy tomorrow.

Aunt Ethel stood up and put out her hand for the letter. "I'm glad he's coming. 'Coming home,' he says, 'home.' But he's getting a round-trip ticket—and he doesn't know that it's all decided now. They'll take our farm and build their dam. Now we'll have to talk about it together, about what we're going to do."

At the school assembly the next day, Aunt Ethel and Uncle Perry came to hear Josiah recite his poem, and to gather with their neighbors.

"'Two roads diverged in a yellow wood,'" he began, and before he knew it he was at the end: "'I took the one less traveled by, / And that has made all the difference.'"

He saw Aunt Ethel and Uncle Perry clapping, and he wondered what roads they would take together. All the roads would lead away from the Swift River Valley, but where would they take him?

Epilogue

It took over ten years to build the reservoir. The value of all the buildings—houses, barns, mills, factories, hotels, train stations, and sheds—was decided on by state appraisers, and slowly each piece of property was purchased, often for less than the owners thought fair. The buildings were demolished and then burned, except for a few that were moved out of the Swift River Valley. All the trees were cut down, and the piled branches and other vegetation were burned. The bodies in the cemeteries were relocated to a new cemetery.

Meanwhile, the dam, a dike, and a tunnel were constructed. In 1938 the final farewell came for the towns of Enfield, Greenwich, Dana, and Prescott and the smaller villages, and in July 1939 the Quabbin Reservoir began to fill. Slowly the water backed up behind the dam and the dike and covered the Swift River Valley.

The land taken by the Commonwealth of Massachusetts has become an "accidental wilderness" inhabited by moose, bears, deer, coyotes, and other animals. Fish swim in its waters and eagles fly over them.

If you look at a map of Massachusetts, you will see a great, blue handprint somewhat west of the middle of the state—that is the Quabbin. The reservoir takes its name from a Nipmuck word meaning "a place of many waters."

Acknowledgments

Without the influence of my father, John E. Rogerson, and the tales he told of the farm he knew as a boy in the 1920s, this book would never have been written.

I am grateful for the support of my husband, my three daughters, and all eight of my grandchildren. Special thanks go to my daughter Josette Haddad for her patience and her excellent copyediting, and to my granddaughter Sonja Ventura for her help with Uncle Albert.

I first took my writing seriously at long-ago meetings of the SCBWI group in Hatfield, MA, under the guidance of Jane Yolen. My appreciation goes also to my writers' group, whose members critiqued early chapters of this book. In addition, I thank my long-running art critique group for their support.

I was encouraged along the way by Susan Rossen, Vee Lyons, Brian Kitely, Margo Culley, and many others.

Last but not least, the experience of living on an old farm in Wendell, MA, with brooks that feed the West Branch of the Swift River and land that abuts land that was taken to protect the Quabbin watershed, has left its mark.

For further understanding of what was lost, visit the Swift River Valley Historical Society in New Salem, MA. And for what the valley has become, visit the Quabbin Reservoir itself.

Helen R. Haddad
hrhaddad@juno.com